I0817782

A Song of Three Spirits

By J. Zachary Pike

Illustrated by Tayla Olandim
Edited by Courtney Rae Andersson
Published by Gnomish Press, December 2018

Version 2.0.0

Gnomish Press, LLC
P.O. Box 64
Greenland, NH 03840

CONTENTS

STAVE I:

UNWELCOME VISITORS

The accounting office buzzed with whispered rumors and desperation. Fenrir Goldson was about to visit. The ancient Dwarven miser comprised half of the Goldson Baggs Group Incorporated's eponymous founders, and by all accounts the less agreeable half. That he should be visiting the accountants in their offices, down near the fifth floor of the main Goldson Baggs office—and on Life's Eve, no less—was raising a panic among the number crunchers and coin counters.

Goldson, for his part, took a moment at the door to listen to the frenzy. The office itself was a taupe cube lined with pine filing cabinets and filled with rows of identical desks. Normally its occupants sat and labored in determined silence, but now they all stood in a circle near the front door, tossing theories and worries back and forth. Was Mr. Goldson coming to announce layoffs? A high-profile firing? Wage cuts or lost bonuses? Had the draft reports been concerning, or worse, incorrect? All parties felt certain that Mr. Goldson would not come down to the fifth floor unless something bad was about to happen.

The old Dwarf was inclined to agree with the prevailing theory; usually, he tried not to interact with the staff unless catastrophe necessitated doing so. But Baggs was gone, and so Goldson was alone on the eve of Mordo Ogg's Day, when business was slower than the god of death himself. Lacking diversion, Goldson had searched for some nit to correct throughout his empire. He found it in the accounting department.

The miserly magnate cleared his throat from the door—the side door, the one that the accountants had paid no heed to while they watched the main entrance—and allowed himself a small smile as terrified whispers gave way to an even-more-terrified silence. Goldson clomped into the room, the fine rings in his long, snowy beard jangling with every stomp of his designer boots. His suit, sharp and crisp and black as coal, contrasted with the saggy, pale, liver-spotted form it was draped over. The room was as quiet as a tomb, and only a little warmer.

"Afternoon," the old Dwarf growled, omitting the good. "I trust you all know that it is the thirtieth of Fadelight, the last day of Fula's month, and that you recognize the significance of that date."

The accountants nodded cautiously. A bold and foolish Human piped up. "It's Life's Eve, sir."

"Bah! Hogwash!" snapped Goldson.

The fool pressed on. "It is, sir! Tomorrow is Mordo Ogg's Day!"

"That's irrelevant!" snapped Goldson. "Mordo Ogg's Day is just like any other day to me, whether or not you lot throw a silly festival. Or it would be just like any other day, were it not the end of the third quarter."

"S-sir, I thought today was the end of the third quarter," suggested another accountant.

"Of course not!" snorted Goldson. "The fourth quarter does not start until next month. Molner's month. So tomorrow is scheduled to be the end of the third."

Mordo Ogg's Day had no month, or was a month of its own, depending on how one looked at a day planner. There may have been some deep symbolism behind this ambiguity within Arth's calendar, but Goldson was solely interested in its implications for the fiscal year. "You have one more day to finalize the quarterly reports. I told the investors they would see those figures no later than the first of the new quarter. And yet, as I looked through the schedule, I was surprised to discover that all of you aim to take the day off!"

Several accountants failed to suppress their groans, their worst fears confirmed.

"But sir!" said the brave Human. "It's a royal holiday!"

"So it is," grumbled the old Dwarf. "I'm legally obligated to pay you time and a half, because the king and the temples have seen fit to interfere with business yet again. Perhaps some among you have enough character to work half as hard again to make up the deficit." He looked over the Humans, Gnomes, and Dwarves huddled in the middle of the room. "Not that I have much hope of that."

"But... but sir! We were to have the day off! What of tradition?"

"What of it?" demanded Goldson.

"You know, deck the halls with red and white, and hide the black for Mordo Ogg? My wife made straw fermals for all the children, and we'll burn them when it's time to darken the lanterns and watch the fireworks! And we're to have tea cakes and presents, and mock griffin pie! It's Mordo Ogg's Day!"

The only sound in the room was a collective shuffle as every other accountant took a step away from the Human.

"What is your name?" hissed Mr. Goldson.

"Brock Ratchet," said the accountant. He was of average height for a Human, just a head above

Goldson, with a clean-shaven face. One of his eyes was brown, the other more gray.

"Ratchet, eh?"

"My father was a Gnome, sir."

"Well, Mr. Ratchet, while I'm handing out free paychecks for layabouts, is there any other luxury that I can heap upon you?" Goldson asked with mock concern. "Perhaps another way I can make your employment less taxing?"

"Actually, sir," said Ratchet, "I've been meaning to inquire about the healing plan."

Few things genuinely surprised Goldson at his age, but the audacity of this young accountant managed to do so. "What?"

"Well, since you mentioned, it's just that I've been making regular payments to the healing plan for five years now, sir. I must say, it never seemed a very good one compared to some companies, but Mrs. Ratchet pressed upon me that it would be prudent to invest in a little something in case of emergencies. And right she was, my dear wife! For now our boy is sick—cursed, really, though the end's the same. He grows weak, and the Temple of Oppo can't help. I tried taking him to one of the really good healers at the Temple of Musana, but that magic's expensive, sir. A healing would cost almost what I make in a year! When I found out, I put in for the Goldson Baggs company healing plan to help cover the cost, but the plan administrators turned me down. They said since the boy has an auspicious birthmark he must have had a predestined condition, and those aren't covered anymore!"

Ratchet shook his head. "I couldn't believe it. I asked them when that sort of thing started to matter, and the administrators gave me the usual speeches about budget cuts and controlling expenses. I don't mind saying that I was floored, sir. I mean, I'm used to dealing with expense reductions when we want coal for the fire or extra ink for the pots, but this is my son! So, I was hoping that, you know, with your position... well, maybe you could help sort it out?"

As Mr. Goldson listened, he could feel his veins bulging out from his papery skin. His jaw clenched so tight that the platinum and gold teeth in his mouth ground sparks off one another. By the time the accountant made his request, the old Dwarf's anger had finally burned through his shock. "Mr. Ratchet! I'll pass along my condolences for your son, but if I hear another word about your wretched life I'll pass along a termination slip instead! Your personal matters are no business of mine, and if you wish to have a job at a business of mine, you'll leave them at home!"

"Ah, yes sir," said the crestfallen accountant. He scurried back a few steps.

"Now, I cannot make you lot work tomorrow," growled Mr. Goldson, eyeing each of the employees in turn. "The choice, by the king's thrice-cursed design, is yours. But I will say that twenty copies of the final quarterly reports are due on my desk the day after tomorrow. And if they are not there come that morning, your desks will be empty by noon! Am I clear?"

Muted assent rippled through the accountants.

"Then I suggest you see to it promptly!" snapped Goldson. By the time he had stomped out the door, the accountants were already back at their desks, quills furiously scribbling across parchment.

Goldson rolled out of the office like a thundercloud, paying no mind to the wreckage in his wake. There were other matters to attend to, and it was already late in the afternoon. He returned to his office to fetch his briefcase and his cloak, then told his assistant to summon the carriage. Within a quarter hour, he was riding through the city in a chamber of velvet and ebony, watching the streets of Andarun pass by through a small window.

The city was encrusted with Mordo Ogg's Day decorations. Evergreen wreaths and paper lanterns hung from the lampposts. People had tied red and white ribbon to every available protrusion from the signposts and gates. Holly sprigs lined the windows of the buildings they passed. Occasionally Goldson caught a glimpse of ebony figurines or charcoal candles in the windows; custom held that one black decoration should be hidden in each house to represent the god of death himself.

"Hogwash!" Goldson snorted to himself again. He wished that Baggs was in the carriage with him.

The carriage moved onto the descending cart lane of the Broad Steps. Buildings flew by on his right; on the left, most of his view was of a plain slab of stone, the Wall that marked the city's eastern border. Down in the middle and lower tiers, the massive edifice loomed higher than Goldson could see from the carriage window. A lost civilization had built the huge barrier in ages long past, as well as the great steps in its shadow, and indeed most of the tiered city wedged into the southern slopes of Mount Wynspar.

As the carriage descended past the sixth tier, the buildings changed. Their facades were more weatherworn, their streets grimier and more covered in detritus, their decorations less thick and vibrant. By the time the carriage pulled off the steps and onto the fourth tier, most of the buildings were sparse brick affairs with chipped paint on their shutters and odd bends in their black iron gates.

Goldson pulled his cloak around himself tightly and glowered at the shabby buildings. His scowl only deepened as the carriage rolled up to an old shop front on Grain Ridge Way. The shutters on the second-floor windows were freshly painted, but shut tight. Its brickwork had been patched and repaired in many places. The building and gate had no Mordo Ogg's Day decorations, or any decoration at all save for gilded lettering on its shop front window that proclaimed it was an office of Goldson Baggs Group Incorporated.

A gaggle of professional heroes lounged around the entryway. A wizard and a cleric, by the look of their outfits, snapped to attention as the carriage door opened. An Elven ruffian wearing a hodgepodge of metal armor and heavy furs didn't bother to straighten up as Goldson creaked down the step and onto the cobblestones.

"Mr. Goldson!" said the cleric, a Human woman in silver chainmail. "I am Mirnen MacLeod, party lead for tonight's job. And this is our wizard, Avalon Tarunin. He's a noctomancer with a lot of experience in these matters. Our warrior there is Zeerith of House Illistyneth, though I doubt we'll need his services. This sort of thing isn't exactly his specialty, as I'm sure you can—"

"Yes, yes, fine." The Dwarf ignored the heroes and turned to a Gnome wearing a black suit with a

Goldson Baggs pin. "Have the preparations been made?"

The assistant assured him that all was according to specifications.

"Then stick to the plan, and make sure the help here doesn't get too familiar. They've a job to do, and it doesn't involve yammering to me." Goldson finally glanced at the cleric on the last word, and then pushed past the incredulous adventurers as briskly as his brittle frame would allow.

Any thought of the unprofessional heroes fled his mind when he arrived at the knocker on the front door. Something was amiss with the old brass hardware. It was carved into a Dwarven face, with the ring suspended from the handles of its mustache. Yet when he looked at it more closely…

The old Dwarf took a handkerchief from his pocket and wiped the offending smudge from the knocker's brow. With the problem fixed, he decided to have the housekeeper fired and pushed his way into the old office.

The building was narrow and dark. Heavy drapes were drawn over all the windows on the old shop front. The ground floor still had the same old desks and chairs that he remembered, though they were piled with strange devices and shrouded in gloom.

Goldson ignored them and made for the narrow staircase to the second-floor landing. Baggs had lived here when they first met, and the living spaces upstairs were well-preserved, though not well used. The steps creaked and groaned as he climbed, and the floor of the landing protested just as loudly as he shuffled past the bedroom and the water closet toward the study.

A pleasant fire burned within the room, and the servants had set a light supper out. The old Dwarf reviewed the sales numbers while he ate, and then settled down with a ledger in the larger of the two chairs by the fire. The hours drained away as he reviewed figures and adjusted planned expenditures.

The sun had long set when he heard a noise from below, a metallic rattle like the joints of chains moving about. Presumably, the cleric and wizard were finalizing their preparations on the first floor. "Thrice-cursed heroes," Goldson muttered to himself. "How am I to concentrate while they make a racket down there?"

But a few moments later, the rattling moved to the stairs, and was now accompanied by the heavy thudding of ascending steps.

A prick of fear penetrated the Dwarf's leathery soul. "Hello? What is that?" he shouted. "Who's there?"

The clanking grew louder as something shuffled toward the door. Goldson's eyes were locked on the entryway, searching for some sign of the visitor. "Cleric? Wizard? What are you about?"

A crack and a flare from the fireplace caught the old banker's attention. He looked and saw that it was just a log shifting. When he turned back to the door, he let out a shout.

A figure stood in the entryway, pale and rotund. Bolbi Baggs, Goldson's old business partner, was wrapped in silver and bronze chains from head to toe.

"Oh, be quiet," said Baggs. "And give me a hand with these. They're quite heavy."

"Baggs!" cried Goldson. "You gave me a fright. You look like a ghost."

"I'd say I look more like I just lugged these heavy chains up the stairs." The Halfling shook a fistful of the medallions hanging off him. He was old, though not as old as Goldson. The curly hair atop his head and feet was snowy white, and the paunch in his fine red coat sagged more than it once had, but his wry smirk was as full of mischief as it had ever been.

"Balderdash!" snapped Goldson. "You were trying to frighten me. I didn't expect you for another hour still."

"I skipped the board meeting and had the servants take me to the Gods' Bazaar up on the sixth tier," said

Baggs. "Seeing you go even paler than usual was merely a side benefit of being early."

"You skipped the board meeting?"

"Canceled it, I should say," said Baggs. "I wanted to see the clerics, as I thought we could use some extra defenses this evening."

Goldson squinted at the silver and gold medallions hanging from his partner. They were carved with sunbursts, eagles, acorns, lanterns, and other objects sacred to Arth's diverse pantheon. "Good gods, man! Are those holy symbols?"

"At least one from every temple. I thought we'd hang them about the beds tonight, as another precaution." The Halfling held up a fistful and grinned at his partner. "I must look quite the pious priest, carrying all of these."

"You look a fool."

"Those aren't mutually exclusive," laughed Baggs.

"Fair enough, but it's all the more reason not to bother with your totems and talismans." Goldson gave a snort and returned to working in his ledger.

"Come now, Goldson! Tonight we are to be haunted by three spirits! The wizards have foreseen as much, and all of the diviners on staff agree. If we're to risk an encounter with the supernatural, why not hedge with a chance for some divine protection? Help me hang these up."

The ancient Dwarf waved his partner away. "Have the help do it."

"The maids and valets are on holiday." The Halfling practically spat the last word.

"There are heroes in the courtyard, and one assistant or another."

"They should stay there. Do you truly want those moldering dunderheads stamping their boots on our polished entwood floors? Dragging their swords past the artwork in the hallway and bedroom?" asked Baggs. "Come on, it won't take but a few minutes."

Goldson complied, but he did so with profuse muttering and swearing. Not half of the medallions had been draped on their bedposts when the old Halfling finally snapped. "Come now, you old Goblin! This minor protection is the least we can do!"

"I can think of a multitude of lesser things to do!" snapped the Dwarf. "And all of them more enjoyable than this sort of manual labor!"

The argument would have continued—indeed, it would have wound through the entire chore if Goldson had his druthers—but it was interrupted by a knock and a voice at the front door. "Uncle? Uncle Bolbi?"

Mr. Baggs rolled his eyes. "Oh, gods, is that—?"

"Uncle!" came the cry again from below, accompanied by an even more vigorous knocking. "Uncle! It's me, Fredegar!"

"It's your thrice-cursed nephew!" hissed Goldson.

"Just be silent and remain still," whispered Baggs. "For all he knows, we're at one of the other offices. He'll go away if he thinks us gone."

Goldson nodded in agreement. He stood transfixed, a medallion of Musana still dangling from his hand, until, to his rising horror, he heard the front door open. "Can I help you?" said a voice within the house.

"Those blasted heroes!" said Baggs. "Who told them to answer the door?"

"Quickly! Stop them!" Goldson dropped the medal and made for the stairs.

They rushed down the steps as quickly as their arthritic bones would allow. The cleric had the front door open, but the old men threw her aside and slammed it shut.

"Uncle? I saw you there!" called the voice outside.

With a long sigh and a withering glare at the cleric and wizard, Baggs opened the door a crack. "Yes?" he said.

"Good cheer, Uncle!" said the portly Halfling on the doorstep. "Happy Life's Eve! Happy Mordo Ogg's Day! May he find you old and happy, if ever."

"Bah! Hogwash!" said Goldson.

"Freddy," said Baggs, without warmth.

"Oh, hello, Mr. Goldson," said Freddy. "And Uncle Bolbi! How good it is to see you!"

"Is it?"

"Very much, sir." Freddy grinned, and his teeth rattled in the chill of the evening. "May I come in?"

"Why?" asked Goldson.

"Why, to bring you good cheer," said Freddy.

"We have enough," said Baggs, though his face said otherwise.

"And I was going to invite you to our feast tomorrow afternoon," Freddy plowed on. "Mrs. Boulger will be making salt potatoes and roast griffin, and we'll have deep fig tea cakes before we put out the lanterns and go for fireworks."

"Bah, hogwash!" said Goldson. "Such silly traditions are nothing but a waste of our kingdom's resources, if you ask me."

"I did not," said Freddy. "I just invited you to enjoy them with us."

"So much the worse!" snorted the Dwarf.

"What Mr. Goldson means to say," interjected Baggs, "is that since you've joined our firm, we cannot be seen showing you favor. It would not do to have the appearance of nepotism."

"But, sirs! You've already made me your chief counsel."

"All the more reason to avoid giving people the impression that we like you," said Baggs.

"You mean, the impression that you like me more than your other lawyers," Freddy prompted.

"Something like that," said Baggs with a shrug.

Goldson slammed the door before the lawyer could reply. Freddy called out to them a couple more times, but they remained silently behind the door.

The heroes watched the old men with dumbfounded faces. The wizard raised a finger. "Uh, should we—"

"We should not!" hissed Baggs.

"This thrice-cursed season brings every sort of vermin out! We can't have them scurrying about in here," said Goldson.

"I'm sorry, sirs," said the cleric. "I just thought—"

"I just thought we hired professional heroes, not a butler service," said Baggs. "If we want people seen in or out, we will do it ourselves!"

At that moment, there was a stomp on the front step and another clank from the knocker. Goldson threw the door open, ready to deliver another admonishment to young Fredegar, but found himself staring at a stout Dwarf in brown robes and a battered hat. A silver medallion with a laurel of olive leaves—a symbol of the god Oppo— was woven into his black beard.

"Yes?" said Baggs cautiously.

"Do I have the honor of addressing Mr. Goldson and Mr. Baggs?" asked the priest. "Rumor has it that they are in this office tonight."

"They're dead," Goldson tried.

"Really? Surely not. I'm certain the whole city would have heard," said the Dwarf.

"Dead tired, then," said Baggs. "Good night!"

"I am Brother Dorgenson, of the Temple of Oppo." The priest shoved a foot in the door and a business card in Baggs's face. "At this festive time of year, we try to think of the poor and destitute, who suffer greatly."

"I try not to think of them when I wish to be festive," said Goldson. "It dampens the mood."

"But to each his own," added Baggs.

Brother Dorgenson pressed on. "Several of us have organized a collection. Your generous donation will go to food and blankets for the city's homeless."

"I think it shall remain right where it is, thank you," said the Halfling.

"But sirs! On Life's Eve, surely there is room in your hearts for those who have nowhere to stay and nothing to eat?"

"Hogwash!" exclaimed Goldson. "Has Saint Garl's Home for the Poor closed?"

"Thankfully not, sir."

"And what of Saint Rill's Soup Kitchen?" pressed Baggs.

"I work there myself, twice a week."

"Then it seems you should be bothering them instead, if the poor are not sufficiently pampered," said Baggs. "Our corporation has made all of the gifts we can deduct this year."

"I am afraid those charities are very busy, and low on supplies," said Brother Dorgenson.

"It's well enough that our generosity isn't wasted, I suppose," said Goldson. "But there are still many factories and mills willing to pay a day's bread for a day's good labor cleaning spell components or weaving fibers."

"Perhaps, sir, but some cannot work."

"Cannot work! Cannot work!" groused Goldson. "Why, everyone can work with sufficient creativity and motivation! And if your poor folk lack those, we cannot give it to them."

"So you see, we can be of no help at all," said Baggs. "The best we can do is not interfere with them, so that hunger and strife will encourage them to better themselves."

"And all we ask in return is the same respect!" snapped Goldson.

Brother Dorgenson finally surrendered, seeing there was no other option. He bade them a happy Mordo Ogg's Day and retreated.

"Cannot work?" Goldson muttered again as he watched the priest retreat up the street, sticking to the glow of the street lamps. "More like will not work!"

"That is the root of the kingdom's troubles," said Baggs. "Nobody has a sense of personal responsibility anymore."

"Indeed. The common man seems to think the world owes him whatever he wants and needs," said Goldson. "When will the people finally look to themselves to solve their own problems?"

"One can only imagine," murmured Goldson. He had spotted another, more pressing cause for concern. A pack of revelers dressed in red and white was tramping up the road, clutching mugs of hot tea and singing "A Song of Three Spirits" at the top of their lungs.

A sailor set his ship afloat
But as sunset drew near
He noticed two more on the deck
Who hadn't afore been there.

"Why have you come?" he asked them.
"For Mordo Ogg," they replied.
"Three spirits haunt your ship tonight
But two leave with the tide."

"They'll be at the door asking for tea cakes and cocoa any moment," said Baggs.

"We'd best retreat out of earshot," said Goldson.

"Theirs or ours?" chuckled Baggs.

The old Dwarf snapped his fingers. "You there! Warrior. What was your name?"

The big Elf stood a little straighter. "Zeerith. Of House Illistyneth," he said.

"Fine. Get outside, and don't let any more riffraff past the gate again tonight," said Goldson, already climbing the steps.

"We're not to be disturbed until you have news of the mission's success," added Baggs.

They returned to the bedroom and resumed hanging the holy symbols about the furniture until an icon of every god was suspended somewhere in the chamber. Then they took turns changing into their nightgowns and using the water closet before climbing into their respective beds. Goldson set his pocket watch on the small end table between them, and Baggs set a candle next to it.

"Are you ready?" The Halfling pulled on a long nightcap.

"So much as I'll ever be," grumbled the Dwarf. "Let's get this over with." And with a nod to his partner, he rolled over and fell into deep sleep.

STAVE II:

THE FIRST OF THE THREE SPIRITS

"Mr. Goldson. Goldson! Wake up!"

Goldson awoke with a start. Baggs was prodding him with the end of a walking cane from his own bed. "What is it?"

"It's beginning!" said Baggs. "Look!"

Goldson examined the end table. His pocket watch said it was a half hour to midnight. The candle next to it was lit, and what was more, the light was growing. The wick and the wax were enlarging as well, and in a moment the candle stepped off its stick and onto the desk. It took the shape of a Gnome with a flame for a head, but indistinct faces flickered and flashed in the fire, like viewing a crowd through a foggy spyglass. The people within the glow seemed to be singing, and Goldson distinctly heard a verse from "A Song of Three Spirits."

The first ghost is what once was.
He glows as though alight.
For the part of life that's clearest
Is the part that's in hindsight.

The apparition put its hands on its hips as it regarded the two businessmen in turn.

The businessmen, in turn, regarded the animated candle with cautious optimism. "What are you, spirit?" asked Baggs.

"I am the Ghost of Mordo Ogg's Day Past," said the spirit.

"And what have you to do with us?" asked Goldson. "Why haunt a couple of old men?"

"For your welfare!" said the ghost.

"My welfare?" snorted the Dwarf. "I've no need of charity. Send someone more useful!"

But the spirit would not be resisted. It took Goldson and Baggs by their hands, yanking them both from their beds. Instead of slamming into the entwood boards, however, all three passed through the floor and into the darkness below.

Candles flared as they drifted to the floor of the back office. The pinpricks of light illuminated a small desk decorated with holly and spruce and a set of filing cabinets stacked with unlit paper lanterns. Familiar voices wafted in through the door.

"Where are we?" breathed Baggs.

"We're in our fourth tier office, of course," snapped Goldson. "Though it smells like a forest in here."

"No, it's not our office. Not yet." Baggs stared at the door, transfixed. His face was caught between awe and joy as he stepped past the spirit and pushed the front door open.

The room beyond was brightly lit and elaborately decorated. The paint on the front windows read "SACKSHIRE-BAGGS CREDIT UNION," all lit up with Mordo Ogg's Day lanterns and festive candles. A crowd of Gnomes from several clans were dancing merrily in a ring while a band played holiday songs. In the center of the merriment, Goldson recognized Bolbi Baggs, still in the prime of his youth, dancing and laughing harder than any.

"This was long ago," said Goldson.

"Yes," said the elder Baggs. He watched a pretty Halfling in a red dress throw her arms around his younger self. "This was the Life's Eve when I was engaged to be married to Lothelia Sackshire."

One of the musicians, flush with rum punch, plucked a sour note. The warmth drained from Lothelia's countenance in an instant, and she knocked young Baggs off his feet as she whirled around to accost the band.

"Dodged an arrow there," remarked Goldson.

"Perhaps, but at the time I was in love," said Baggs, a bit wistfully. "She had good sense and ran her father's business shrewdly. When we merged our firms, it seemed our hearts merged as well."

Lothelia helped the young Baggs to his feet. The music resumed, though with less merriment and considerably more urgency. The dancing began again. As the newly betrothed Halfling spun across the floor, she leaned close and whispered into his ear. The younger Baggs's grin spread even wider.

"Do you remember that?" prompted the Ghost of Mordo Ogg's Day Past. "Do you remember sweet nothings and loving whispers?"

"Sweet nothings?" scoffed Baggs the elder. "Nothing of the sort! Why, she whispered to me about her success securing deposits from a particular law firm. Look!"

The Halfling's younger self had stopped dancing, and still wearing his enamored smile, proclaimed congratulations to Lothelia for making such an admirable transaction. He added that he himself had secured a meeting with Fenrir Goldson, an up-and-coming investor in the financial world. The news earned him a passionate kiss.

"Uh, right. Right." The ghost's flame faded a little, but it rallied admirably. "You were happy together, and yet look! Just one year later!"

5678

On the last word, all warmth drained from the room, and the partygoers and band faded like mist. The only light left was a lamp set on the front desk and a dim Mordo Ogg's Day lantern that had been left to burn too long. A few sprigs of holly and pine had been scattered around the office.

Young Baggs sat at the illuminated desk, working at a ledger feverishly. A younger Fenrir Goldson stood next to him. The Dwarf still had a head of hair then, almost as long as his beard, and the braids woven in both were only tinged with gray.

"I know this day," said the older Goldson.

"As do I," said Baggs softly.

The front door opened, and Lothelia stormed in. She wore a red dress laced with white, and a crimson snarl laced with veins. "Bolbi!" she shouted. "Are you really still at the books?"

"And why should I not be?" asked the younger Baggs.

"It's Life's Eve!" said his betrothed. "We were to attend a party!"

"So attend it!" said Baggs. "Perhaps you can secure the Gorgon account."

For a moment, it looked as though Lothelia would burst. Yet when she looked to young Goldson and his polite, crocodilian smile, her shoulders fell. "That is it, then. You've made your choice."

"Have I?" asked Baggs.

"Yes. A hundred times this year. This used to be our business. Now you see it as yours, and me as just another worker in it. I was looking forward to our partnership, Bolbi." Lothelia looked from Mr. Baggs back to Mr. Goldson. "But you've found another. This is not my company anymore."

The young Baggs froze, eyes wide. "Does… does that mean you wish to sell out your shares?"

"What?" Lothelia took a step back as though struck.

"For four hundred thousand, perhaps? suggested Goldson. He opened up another desk and produced a thin stack of papers. "We've already had the contracts drawn up."

"For just such a contingency," said Baggs.

"How could you?" asked Lothelia. "How could you think to…"

"We found out about your scheme with the Lamia Sisters," said Baggs. "And now that it's out, this is probably the easiest way to end things."

She stared at him for a moment, a hint of tears in her eyes, and then she dashed forward to grab a quill. Her first signature on the contract was scrawled and passionate, but there were more pages to initial, clauses to be reviewed, a tiny edit to be made to section fourteen, and then a final signature and date. It made for a very long few minutes as she did the paperwork, sobbing. Goldson and Baggs watched the walls awkwardly as she worked. When the contract was done, she took one last look at Bolbi, then fled the office.

"And so she left you—" the Ghost of Mordo Ogg's Day Past began.

He was cut off by a sudden fit of uproarious laughter. Not from the younger Goldson and Baggs, who were grinning ear to ear as they reviewed the freshly executed contract, but from their elders. The old duo chortled as they watched Lothelia flee through the dark streets, snow just beginning to drop on her.

"Oh ho! I had forgotten she was crying!" laughed Baggs. "That makes it more perfect."

"And her face!" wheezed Goldson. "Ha ha! Her face!"

The candle spirit stepped back, and the faces flickering in its flame looked appalled. "You… you find this amusing?"

"It's the most I've laughed in ages," said Goldson.

"Have you no heart, sirs?" said the ghost.

"Heart?" said Baggs. "It was just business. Nothing personal."

"Nothing personal?" the ghost cried. "You were to be married!"

"Oh, Lothelia always wanted a lapdog more than a husband," said the old Halfling, waving dismissively.

"I heard she's had many of both by now," added Goldson, still laughing. "And the dogs last longer! Ha!"

"She wanted to keep me a junior partner, and plotted with the Lamia Sisters to cut Goldson out of the business," Baggs said. "She was always plotting for control, and never stopped either. The marriage was just one scheme in a long list of her machinations."

"She's been a thorn in our side for decades," said Goldson.

"But surely you felt something for her!" protested the ghost. "Surely you had love in you once?"

"Perhaps," said Baggs with a sigh, "but I've outgrown it."

"And now you feel nothing for her?" asked the ghost.

"Respectful aggression, perhaps? Cordial malice? She is the competition," said Baggs. "It feels good to see her schemes fall apart so completely."

"And emotionally!" cackled Goldson. "Gods, her face!"

"Indeed, ha ha!" laughed Baggs. "I'd have paid good gold to see her weep so."

Their merriment continued unabated. The Ghost of Mordo Ogg's Day Past stood between them, its wax nubs balled into tiny fists. And as their guffawing rose, so did the flame on the spirit's head, until it was a furious inferno.

Baggs didn't notice. He wiped his eyes and watched the window where Lothelia had fled. "Here now, spirit, this has been fun, but take us back to our beds. Tomorrow is the end of the quarter, and we have work to do."

"Spirit?" said Goldson, glancing at the flame.

"Another vision!" hissed the ghost. It reached out with both arms and gave a mighty clap.

The room flooded with light, burning away the young partners and the decorations. When the glare faded, a different Goldson and Baggs were in their place, each a little grayer now. The office was decorated with a single wreath of pine needles hung begrudgingly on the door. A portly Gnome in a shabby suit stood before the two businessmen—a Scribkin, by the size of his nose. A presentation card sat forgotten on an easel beside him; all eyes in the room were on a briefcase full of colorful swatches of leather and chainmail set on the desk.

"What is this?" asked old Goldson, a lump of fear rising in his throat.

"What is this?" demanded his younger self, gesturing angrily at the case on the table. "Dyed lacing and painted bits of metal? Why are you bringing this rubbish into our office?"

"What Mr. Goldson means to say," said the younger Baggs, "Is that we expect the Andarun Valve Corporation to make plumbing, Mr. Gabben."

"Y-y-yes, sirs," stammered the Gnome. "B-b-but—"

"Half-pipes and baffles. That sort of thing," said Mr. Baggs. "Not... colored armor."

"P-p-personalization options," said Mr. Gabben, wiping the sweat from his spectacles. "Our market research indicates that p-p-professional heroes will pay a premium for armor and weapons that express themselves and build their br-brands."

"Hogwash! Does your market research tell you what a plumbing company is supposed to make?" bellowed Goldson. "How many scientists does it take to figure out what people want pipe makers to sell?"

The elder Baggs's face suddenly lit up with realization and fear. "Spirit, no more! I wish to see no more!"

"Look on!" hissed the ghost, his flame still raging.

"And so your company has nothing more to offer us than painted armor?" asked Baggs. "That's what you're hoping we'll invest our hard-won gold in?"

"Uh." Mr. Gabben wore the wince of someone who only has one answer and knows that it is the wrong one. "W-we are also working on a line of hats."

"Ridiculous!" hollered Goldson.

"Silly beyond measure!" echoed Baggs.

Barking similar expressions of contempt, the young partners drove the panicked Scribkin from their office without so much as a single wish of a happy Mordo Ogg's Day.

Their older selves groaned at the spectacle.

"Spirit, no more!" said old Goldson. "I beg you! No more visions!"

"One more!" hissed the Ghost of Mordo Ogg's Day Past. It grabbed the two businessmen by the hand and lurched toward the wall. Once again, they passed through the wood instead of colliding with it, but the space on the other side was a far cry from the small alley between the fourth tier office and the clock shop next door. Instead, Goldson and Baggs found themselves in the middle of a ballroom. A small gathering was going on; a cluster of the city's rich and powerful having tea cakes and an herbal brew for Life's Eve.

Lothelia was there. Her red dress had touches of white and green about it, just as her bright eyes had a touch of age about the edges. A small, bluish dog was perpetually around her, though never in the same spot for more than a few seconds. One moment it was at her heel, and another it perched dutifully on her shoulder, and a heartbeat later it was over on the buffet sniffing at the frosted confections. It never ran between these positions, but disappeared with a faint puff of azure smoke and rematerialized elsewhere in an instant.

Mr. Gabben pushed his way from the crowd, wearing a short, misshapen beard that pointed out at all angles. He beamed at Lothelia as he shook her hand. "Miss Sackshire," he said, approaching her with a warm smile. "A happy Mordo Ogg's Day to—oh!"

"Mr. Gabben! Welcome! And don't mind Nala." Lothelia waved away the Gnome's surprise at her dog materializing in his arms. "She wants to be your friend."

"Indeed?" Mr. Gabben craned his neck to maneuver his face away from the dog's frantic licking.

"Oh yes. Flicker Spaniels are very friendly."

The shade of Mr. Goldson's future felt a leaden lump drop in his stomach. "Spirit, do not make us watch this!" he protested.

The Ghost of Mordo Ogg's Day Past stood resolute between Goldson and Baggs, its waxen hands holding them as surely as any vise.

"Very agreeable," remarked Mr. Gabben. He leaned so far back it seemed he would fall over trying to avoid the dog's persistent tongue, but at the last moment Nala disappeared and rematerialized by the punch bowl. The Scribkin righted himself with a smile.

"I must say I'm feeling agreeable as well, given our profits this year."

Lothelia grinned. "Three hundred percent growth does put everything in a festive light, does it not? Your personalized armaments have proven most profitable for both of us!"

"I never dreamed I could be so wealthy!" remarked Mr. Gabben.

"Spirit!" cried Baggs. "Release us! Show us no more!"

"I wonder how you shall top it this year?" Lothelia asked.

"Wait until you see the hats," said Mr. Gabben.

"No more!" shrieked Goldson. He grabbed the nightcap off Baggs's head and pulled it over the Ghost of Mordo Ogg's Day Past, extinguishing its flame.

At Goldson's cry, Lothelia's dog looked up from the punch bowl, directly at the old Dwarf, and barked. The sound twisted and distended like taffy from a puller's hook as the light atop the ghost was snuffed out. Goldson felt for a moment like he was falling, but when he threw out his arms to catch himself, all he felt was a pillow. He sat up in his bed with a cry.

"Goldson!" Baggs's nightcap was back on his head and unsinged, though it was slightly rumpled. "We're back!"

Goldson ignored him. "Did you see that?" he wheezed.

"Every excruciating moment of it. Gods, the opportunity cost of that dreadful deal," gasped Baggs. "Why did you ever doubt Mr. Gabben?"

"Me?" snarled Goldson. "What of you? Why did you not listen to him?"

"No helping it now! Wait a moment!" said Baggs, lighting a new candle. The Halfling leapt from his bed and ran into the hallway, taking the light with him. Goldson heard him thud downstairs, followed by some disappointed muttering. A few moments later, he returned with a fierce scowl on his face. "Nothing!"

"It's the most useless ghost anyway," grumbled Goldson.

"Not so useless as the cleric and the wizard," Baggs snarled as he clambered back into bed. "Mark my words, I'll fire the both of them if we have nothing to show again tomorrow."

"Tomorrow," agreed Goldson, who was feeling very tired. He lay back down and was asleep before his head landed on his pillow.

STAVE III:

THE SECOND OF THE THREE SPIRITS

Mr. Goldson awoke to a medley of delicious aromas. Scents of bacon, pastries, roasted meats, and jellied sweets filled his nostrils. Someone had prepared breakfast, lunch, dinner, and tea as well, by the smell of it.

Someone else, or perhaps the same person who had prepared the food, was singing softly in a rich baritone.

Second comes the present.
He looms larger than his kin,
For the part of life you can't ignore
Is the moment you're now in.

Goldson breathed in deeply, and then gave a sharp cry as his eyes drifted open.

Across the bedroom, wreathed in light, sat a giant of a man; bigger even than a Troll. He had curly hair like a Halfling, but a beard as long as a Dwarf's, and there was something Elven about the twinkle in his eye. He wore a laurel of holly and silverleaf, and a long red robe that was open in the front. His laughter was booming, and grew even deeper when Baggs sat up in bed and cried out as well.

"What the blazes is going on?" shouted Baggs.

"Welcome! Welcome!" thundered the giant, resting easily on a great horn of plenty set atop the couch. "Come! Out of bed and speak with me!"

But Goldson had lost interest in the spirit. Instead, he stared at the floor, wild rage rising in his cracking voice. "Is that a roast pig on our polished entwood? And a tray of jellied pastries on my Imperial rug?"

"Uh…" The ghost's laughter faded a bit as he looked around. The room was filled with every sort of foodstuffs, from roast goose to griffin pie. Yet as plentiful as the feast was, there was a famine of serveware.

"Good gods, man! Did you hang sausages from the bed? These are silk sheets!" hollered the old Dwarf.

"I've stepped in a pie!" cried Baggs. "Why would you set a pie by the bed?"

"I am the Ghost of Mordo Ogg's Day Present!" hollered the spirit, trying to retake command of the conversation.

Goldson would have none of it. "And my fine curtains left to rest in a tray of thrice-cursed bacon! Why would you bring all of this food in here? I can't imagine a more unsanitary thing!"

"Mordo Ogg's Day is a time of celebration and feasting!" boomed the ghost.

"More like excess and waste!" said Baggs, extricating himself from the offending pastry. "There's only three of us, you fool! What are we to do with all this?"

"Oysters?" shrieked Goldson. "Oysters atop my favorite chair!"

"I'd think an immortal spirit should know better," the Halfling chided.

"Aha, but I am just several hours old! For each Mordo Ogg's Day is a new spirit, bound to live but a day—"

"That's not what the cleric said!" snorted Baggs.

"Though I hope it's true," said Goldson. "How else could you be so dull-witted as to drag an entire feast up here for two old men at midnight?"

The Ghost of Mordo Ogg's Day Present sighed and slapped a meaty hand to his great forehead. "It... this is only a vision."

"Well, visions had better not leave stains!" snapped Goldson.

"It won't stain!" growled the ghost. Then, with another deep breath, he managed to regain a measure of his joyful countenance. "I have come to teach you two a lesson through apparitions of this year's Mordo Ogg's Day."

"Yes, we're familiar with this bit by now," said Baggs.

"Then just… just take hold of my robes," said the spirit resignedly.

"And now we've found a more unsanitary thing," grumbled Goldson.

"Take hold of my robes or I shall dump this pudding on your precious rugs!" bellowed the ghost.

The old men grumbled and snarled about it, but they navigated the piles of food set haphazardly throughout their bedroom and touched the ghost's velvet robes. As soon as the fabric was in Goldson's reluctant grasp, the room vanished, edibles and all.

They stood in the streets of Andarun, down by the Base from the look of it. The buildings all appeared to have been cobbled together from older, nicer structures. Only a light dusting of snow fell this far down the mountain. Dawn's light was rising over the Wall, and people of every sort flooded out into the streets, wide grins on their faces. The children dragged fermals, traditional dolls made of straw and rags given out on Mordo Ogg's Day morning. A few were wearing new coats, another routine gift of the season. Parents with weary smiles trailed after them on the way to one temple or another.

Custom pressed the commoners to visit their patron gods on Mordo Ogg's Day, but shrines to the lord of death's gate himself remained largely unrecognized. That was fine by all accounts, even the clergy of Mordo Ogg. After all, most gods needed to produce miracles, inspire scriptures, or start holy wars to get the attention of mortals. The god of death only needed to wait.

The streets quickly became crowded, but today's throngs acted differently. Goblins and Dwarves gave each other friendly nods. Gnomes and Gremlins deferred to one another for places in the temple queues. Elves walked through the streets without looking down on everyone else—at least, not too much. Andarun thrummed with indiscriminate altruism and generosity.

Only two figures among the masses lacked happy faces, and nobody could see them anyway.

"Look at all of these layabouts," groused Goldson. "Every one of them on someone's payroll today, whittling away their employers' fortunes while they fritter away the hours! How much could the kingdom accomplish right now if half of these people were at work, applying themselves to industry?"

"They are taking time from daily distractions to focus upon what is important in life," said the Ghost of Mordo Ogg's Day Present.

"Seems to me that you have that entirely backward," said the old Dwarf.

"I've often wondered why people are so happy on a day dedicated to the god of death," Baggs mused. He was watching a pack of children run through the streets, each carrying a raggedy fermal. "Why so much joy on such a morbid occasion?"

"Death is merely the last part of life," said the ghost. "And so long as you are alive, it is good to remember to make the most of what you have with your time as a mortal."

"That was my point," said Goldson.

The spirit's countenance dimmed a measure. "Industry alone cannot bring you happiness."

"But through work, one earns the things that can!" Goldson retorted.

"Gold alone is not the key to happiness," said the Ghost. "Come! Take my robes and I will show you."

"The other ghost didn't need us to touch anything," Baggs muttered to Goldson.

But they did take hold of the spirit's robes, however reluctantly, and with a great gale the alley blew away. Or perhaps it was Goldson and Baggs that flew; the moment was too disorienting to tell. When the wind died down, however, they were in the main chamber of a small apartment.

The room aspired to be quaint, but there was no escaping that the furnishings were a moldering collection of scavenged pieces. Festive-looking bits of trash had been scattered about—strings of discolored popped corn, bowls of half-melted wax fruit, some scavenged pine needles, a sprig of fabric holly that was worn around all of the edges. Yet the quarters still felt warm and welcoming, if only because of the smiles and laughter of its occupants.

One person in particular struck Goldson. "Good gods! It's Brock Ratchet!"

"Who?" asked Baggs.

"Uppity fellow from the accounting department. I have half a mind to fire him once the quarterly reports are finalized."

"You couldn't if you had half a heart," said the ghost. "Have you ever seen lovelier people?"

Goldson and Baggs looked back to the family. Mrs. Ratchet was a plump matron in a checkered apron, with an easy smile and eyes like sapphires. She was bustling in the kitchen, assisted by four Humans in various states of youth. They teased each other and giggled together as they put colored frosting and dried fruits on a platter of eight neat tea cakes.

Brock tended the fire with an old poker. "Here now, Bellagail, how are those cakes coming along?"

"If they taste as good as they look, we'll be talking of them all year!" exclaimed Mrs. Ratchet. "Marta, hand me those dried apples. And Peta, make sure you save the black frosting for Mordo Ogg's cake!"

"Yes, mum!" said the two eldest children in unison.

"I suspect we'll have the feast soon, then," said Brock. "A good meal in my belly will get me through my reports quickly, and then I'll be home in time for gifts and fireworks!"

"They do seem a rather pleasant family," Baggs remarked to Goldson.

"Ah! The office on Mordo Ogg's Day!" said Mrs. Ratchet, a scowl twisting her face. "A pox on that wicked Mr. Goldson for making you work!"

"Of a sort," Goldson said through gritted teeth.

"Mrs. Ratchet!" protested Brock. "It's Mordo Ogg's Day!"

"Too right!" said his wife. "What a wicked day to make men work! What a day to slave away for those tyrants!"

"What a day to bear no man ill will," Brock said. "Life is too precious to waste on malice."

"Too short to waste on the likes of your wretched employer, anyway," she replied. "Do they care nothing for this day?"

"They're paying time and a half," said Brock. "And Mr. Goldson cared quite a lot regarding that."

"I'll bet the old miser did." Mrs. Ratchet waved away the thought. "But fair enough. Life is too short for grudges. Besides, the pie is ready, and the tea cakes are setting."

"I'll go get him, then?" said Mr. Ratchet.

"If he's ready," said Bellagail.

He headed off into the back room and emerged shortly thereafter with a small boy holding a wooden crutch. "Come along, little Lance," he said softly. "Look! Your Mum has made you a right feast for Mordo Ogg's Day!"

The child turned to look upon his family's labors, prompting the shades of Goldson and Baggs to take a step back. Little Lance had a pleasant countenance, with a gentle smile and big, kind eyes. But the middle of his forehead bore a blue and purple mark in the unmistakable shape of a skull. The tiny apparition stared out from the boy's forehead in a way that had both Goldson and Baggs convinced that it was looking directly at them.

"Well, that..." The old Dwarf wiped sweat from his brow. "That is certainly an auspicious birthmark. One can hardly blame the administrators of the company healing plan for not wishing to be held accountable for financing his treatment."

"Curses and portents of that sort are quite expensive to treat, I hear," said Baggs.

"Exorbitantly," said Goldson. "Though I suppose it's hardly fair to blame the boy, either, just for being born with such a mark."

"It seems there is nobody to blame," said the ghost. "And yet, if nobody alters their course, the child will not see another Mordo Ogg's Day."

"Surely not!" said Baggs. "There are temples and poor houses to give him aid."

"They are full," said the ghost. "And they lack the gold for the expensive magic he requires."

"Then the kingdom shall step in," said Goldson, looking up at the tall spirit. "Gods knows they are always draining our coffers to fund their public health projects."

The ghost shook its great head. "All are underfunded, since King Handor cut your corporate taxes yet again. How could they handle such a costly curse as the boy's without more resources?"

"You see?" Baggs said to Goldson. "This is why the kingdom should not be charged with healing its citizens. The bureaucrats and kingdom arbiters have no solutions but to tax those of us who actually labor!"

"Quite right. The kingdom never offers a good solution," agreed Goldson. "So once again, it all comes back to personal responsibility."

"Perhaps. The question is, which persons?" the ghost asked pointedly.

Goldson was taken aback. "Are you suggesting that we might have a part in the child's misfortune?"

"Something like that," muttered the ghost. "But whatever the past, it now stands that you, personally, could finance the healing the child needs to be well. Either of you could easily afford his treatment."

"Not as easily as you can speak of it," Baggs shot back. "Besides, even if we did give the Ratchets gold for the boy's treatment, they wouldn't have earned it. They won't learn to overcome circumstance through grit and sweat! What about the next calamity to befall them? And the next after that? If they lack the character to overcome this hardship, surely the next will claim them."

"He has a point," said Goldson. "No one gift, no single chance delivered out of the sky, can change the true nature of a man. No matter how great an opportunity to better himself you give him, his character will always shine through."

The ghost gave them a sidelong glance from above.

"What?" asked Goldson. "I am merely saying that Mr. and Mrs. Ratchet must take their circumstances upon themselves. If this family's moral fiber is anything such as you claim, they will find a way to help the boy."

"Yes! Exactly," said Baggs. "Let us hope and pray for that."

The Halfling's comments elicited a pang of worry in old Goldson. Mr. Baggs only called upon the gods to intervene when all available mortals had opted not to. If he was making declarations of piety already, it was as dire an omen for little Lance as the morbid birthmark upon his brow. And despite the fact that Goldson was not fond of many people, even his ancient heart was not sufficiently calcified to completely resist the boy's good-natured innocence.

The child himself had hobbled to the table and joined in the children's whispered excitement regarding the forthcoming feast. "Are we really to have griffin, Father?" he asked Brock.

"Next best thing; your mom's made a mock griffin pie," said Mr. Ratchet.

"Mock griffin? What's a thrice-cursed mock griffin pie?" asked Baggs, and little Lance echoed the question without the obscenity.

"Well, our Peta found an old alley cat that got hit by a carriage," said Mr. Ratchet. "And clever Marta snared a fat pigeon in the park last evening."

"Good gods!" exclaimed Goldson.

"A little tinderspice, a pinch of nutmeg, and nobody can tell the difference between it and real griffin!" declared Mrs. Ratchet, setting a golden pie on the table.

"I'll wager I could," said Baggs.

"I'd pay just to see you eat it," Goldson told him.

The Ratchet family, however, was genuinely delighted by the meat pie, along with the roasted tubers and wilted green salad that were placed on the table. Little Lance looked particularly excited. "Oh, Mother! It looks delightful! I've never seen such a magnificent feast! It will be a wonder if I ever see it's equal!"

Brock Ratchet smiled in a way that made Goldson's stomach turn. There was a tremor in Mr. Ratchet's voice as he whispered, "Let us hope you do."

With that, they sat down to dinner. Lance asked to say a few words before they ate. He cleared his throat and spoke as loudly and boldly as his condition would allow. "On this Mordo Ogg's Day, let us thank the gods for the life we've been given."

"Such a good boy!" said Mrs. Ratchet.

"We're grateful to Maeneth for all the food we have received," piped the boy. "We thank Dakran and Oppo for all of their generosity. And we praise Fulgen for hope of even better days."

Mr. Ratchet smiled at his wife. "He always does mind the priests at temple."

"We wish the All Mother health, and pray that her mind will one day be whole again. And until that day, we thank Tandos for his steady hand, and ask for his continued protection."

"May it be so," said all of the other children in unison.

Suddenly, the mark on Lance's forehead glowed green. His big, brown eyes rolled back in his head, and light shone out from their sockets, his mouth, and his nostrils. *"And when the Deceiver sits upon the highest throne, the darkness grasps the world in a fist made of iron and gloved in silk. It shall root out our last hopes and consume our souls as it crushes the bones of the world!"* he intoned in a voice far beyond his years.

"That's a bit much, dear," said Mrs. Ratchet.

The light left Lance's face, and the skull shape on his brow faded as he shook his head. "Sorry, Mother."

"That mark does seem quite serious," said Goldson, watching the boy clutch his forehead.

"Let us hope and pray that someone does something, then." The Ghost of Mordo Ogg's Day Past stared at Goldson and Baggs with eyes that burned like coals.

"Indeed," said Baggs uncomfortably.

The prayer at the table, at least, was over and done. The family ate their meat pie and vegetables with gusto. A glow of familial joy hung over them as they laughed and ate. In between the meat pie and dessert, little Lance suggested that they all sing Mordo Ogg's Day songs. They broke out in choruses of "Gods Rest Ye, Fairy Gentlemen" and "A Song of Three Spirits."

"Is there a point to watching a family of paupers eat?" Baggs asked as Mrs. Ratchet served the spiced apple pudding. "Are we expected to suffer through the entire meal?"

"There is more to be seen!" boomed the giant ghost. In a much quieter voice he added, "And if you suffer, so much the better."

"What?"

"Look!" the spirit exclaimed at the top of his voice. "See, the merriment is cut short!"

They looked. Brock was standing and muttering apologies and love to all of his dear children. "I shan't be long," he told them. "You can play with your fermals when the plates are clear, and I'll be home in time for presents and fireworks."

"Do you promise you'll be back before we go to bed, Father?" asked little Lance.

Mr. Ratchet smiled bravely, but a glittering around his eyes evidenced his tears as he kissed his youngest's head. "I have but a few reports to see to, and I will work my hardest to have them done before your supper, my boy. That's all I can promise, but I promise you that."

The other children groaned in disappointment. Little Lance nodded and hugged his father tight.

"And what do you make of that?" the ghost rumbled as Mr. Ratchet put on his cloak and top hat.

"I suppose Mr. Ratchet has a better work ethic than I appreciated," said Goldson, stroking his long beard.

"Is that all?" demanded the spirit.

Baggs stared up at the giant in consternation. "What else should there be?"

The ghost's patience finally broke. "Some guilt! Some shame! It is because of you that this man cannot spend Mordo Ogg's Day with his family!"

"It is not us!" protested Goldson. "It's the investors! The competition!"

"If we cannot keep our edge, the markets will flee from the Goldson Baggs Group to more aggressive firms," said Baggs. "Our company's stock will plummet."

"We'll lose business," chimed in Goldson.

"And then people will lose jobs!" said Baggs with a firm nod.

"Why, the Ratchets and their children would be out on the streets with the wretches," said Goldson.

The ghost's great brow rose in apparent skepticism. "So even though his labors profit you most, it is for his sake that you bid him work through the holiday."

"His, and many more workers," said Baggs, watching Brock bid his sons and daughters goodbye. "We are caretakers to the gainful employment of thousands."

"We take that duty seriously," said Goldson.

"And we are compensated in accordance!" added Baggs.

"How fortuitous of you to make your riches taking responsibility for a man's job without being responsible for the hardships it inflicts upon him," said the ghost.

"You know nothing of our work!" the Dwarf fired back. "You're half a day old, and you think you can speak of the sacrifices we've made?"

"Why, consider that I am not spending Mordo Ogg's Day with my family either," said Baggs.

"Perhaps. But you have gained much more from your time away than Mr. Ratchet will," said the ghost. He looked back at the Ratchet family putting on brave smiles as they waved goodbye to their husband and father. "And I suspect that you have given up much less in missing out on your family."

"How dare you?" snorted Baggs. "I resent the implication!"

"Do you?" said the ghost. "Take hold of my robes and let us visit your nephew, then."

"Uh, well..." With his bluff called, Bolbi Baggs wore a rare expression of speechlessness. "I am sure we do not need to see—"

"Come!" demanded the ghost, taking Goldson and Baggs by the sleeves. The Ratchet's home became a blur, and a blast of snow and ice whipped past. Another moment, and they were in a different home.

The chamber they stood within was a warm and spacious expanse, dominated by a great stone fireplace with a flame drake's head mounted above the mantle. The furniture was carved from rich woods and covered in fine upholstery. Wreaths hung from every door, and paper lanterns were placed on every windowsill. A table was set with tea cakes for the afternoon, but the confections were in no immediate danger; the scent of roast meat still hung in the air, and the Halflings seated round the fire held their generous bellies in satisfaction.

"Oh, that was a glorious feast, my dear!" exclaimed Fredegar Boulger.

"Did everybody get enough to eat?" asked his wife.

A chorus of assent rose from the other Halflings.

"You know we all did," laughed Freddy. "Why, if anything, there might have been too much food!"

"No harm in having too much," said his wife. "There will be leftovers for second breakfast now, and we can share some with the servants when they come tomorrow. Besides, you told me I'd have two more guests!"

"Ha! Perhaps I did, my dear, but I doubt dear Uncle Bolbi and Mr. Goldson could enjoy as much as you made for them."

"I doubt those two could enjoy anything," groused a Halfling seated next to Mrs. Boulger. "That pair could make a fireworks show miserable. Why, I've never heard of such a thoroughly unpleasant duo."

"Who's that wretch?" Goldson demanded of Baggs.

"Otho Sackshire," his partner sighed. "One of Lothelia's sons by her third or fourth husband, and the brother-in-law of my foolish nephew. Perhaps you were right, spirit, and I have not lost so much by missing this."

But at that point, young Freddy interrupted Otho's grousing. "Now that really is enough! I admit my uncle and his partner have their eccentricities, but they're living souls and deserving of kindness on Mordo Ogg's Day, if no other!"

"Didn't you say Mr. Goldson called Mordo Ogg's Day hogwash?" asked a young woman sitting across from Freddy.

"Why give them goodwill when they do not believe in it?" asked Otho with a smirk.

"The season's charity is indiscriminate, and for a purpose," said Freddy. "Besides, why begrudge a heart that cannot find joy? I feel only pity for my uncle and Mr. Goldson."

"I've no need of his pity!" snapped Goldson.

"Surely not." Baggs smiled at his nephew. "But at least I can say that he's still a loyal and good lad."

"If you only pity the pair, then why shackle yourself to working for them?" asked Otho, his shrewd eyes narrow.

"Oh, my uncle has been most generous in making me his counsel," said Freddy. "And he gave me a salary big enough that Mrs. Boulger and I have everything we need and more."

"Perhaps, but that is all in the past," said Otho. "You already have the title of general counsel, and having given you that, your uncle can't even spare an hour or so to eat your food. Do you really think he'll give you a raise or make you a partner in his firm?"

"Now that does ring true," said Mrs. Boulger, with a pointed look to Freddy.

"But he is my dear Uncle Bolbi!" protested Fredegar. "Last of my sweet mother's generation! He's family!"

"Are you so dear to him?" asked Otho. "Was he regretful when he declined to come to Mordo Ogg's Day dinner? Did he offer to visit another time? Or present you with a counter-invitation?"

Fredegar said nothing, but sank back into his seat. He swirled his brandy as he stared thoughtfully into the fire.

"I thought not," said Otho, not unkindly. "You'll do as you see fit, I'm sure, but were I in your place I would be leveraging that title of yours for a partnership at some firm or another."

"Perhaps," said Freddy with a shrug.

"How loyal is the boy, exactly?" Goldson said, arching an eyebrow at Baggs.

"I made you, you ungrateful wretch!" Baggs hollered at his nephew. "I paid for your schooling! I donated to your college! I hired you on your graduation day into a title most work years for! And this is how you thank me? By considering this… this slanderous plotting?"

Baggs's nephew, of course, couldn't hear a word of his uncle's rant. Yet he did sit up suddenly, as though jolted. "But hear now, that's enough business talk," Freddy cried with a renewed smile. "This is a time for happier thoughts. Let's have us a game, shall we?"

His guests agreed, and a pair of them helped Freddy fetch a card table. The Halflings settled down to a game of Wust's Kettle.

Freddy won a few hands, and Otho had a run of bad luck, but the talk of the game was Mrs. Boulger's string of success. She was starting to drop hints about making the kettle more interesting by tossing in some gold when Freddy pointed out the window. "Look! The shadows are falling, and it's almost time to dim the lanterns. We should have tea, if we're going to. Come! Come! Call the children!"

Shouts went up the stairs to come down for tea. A great rumbling emerged from the ceiling, moving like a thunderous poltergeist from the spot above the table toward the staircase. Five young Halflings, curly-haired and rosy-cheeked, dashed down the steps, followed by an ungainly Human that smacked his head against the lintel at the bottom of the stairs. One of the Halfling women rushed over to comfort the boy, who was easily half-again her height.

Goldson shot Baggs a questioning look.

"I'd heard Otho's sister Polla has a predilection for Elves," said Baggs. "So much so that she went and had a Human with one of them. It was quite a scandal a few years back."

"Come along, Jebby. You're all right," said the Human's mother. They joined the others at the table, where they were welcomed with tea cakes and smiles.

"Doesn't seem like anybody minds now." said Goldson.

"Oh, I hear a comment about Polla or the boy now and then," said Baggs. "But not to their faces, and not at this time of year."

"Mordo Ogg's Day brings out the best in all sorts of folk!" boomed the ghost. "It reminds everyone of what they should be."

"Should be?" snorted Goldson. "Why should they be anything but what they are? Why labor to be what you're not?"

"How else should people better themselves?" said the ghost. "You work hard to improve your finances, your stature, your influence. Why should the improvement of your character be effortless?"

"You presume this is a real improvement," smirked Baggs, watching his family settle in at the table. "I know them better. I've seen the way they jockey for status and praise. This entire party is nothing but another competition to show who is the most inundated with holiday spirit. It's all for the sake of being admired in tomorrow's gossip."

"Showing others their festivity does not preclude them from actually being festive," said the ghost.

"Their motives may not be everything you wished, but they are at their best this time of year."

Baggs shrugged at that, and his lips scrunched up in a manner that usually meant he was thinking hard about something. "Perhaps," he said, watching his family.

Young Jebby got an extra large teacake, and he had to sit on his knees instead of getting one of the Halfling-sized chairs, but otherwise he was treated no different than any of the other children. After tea, the adults poured themselves a round of brandy and toasted Clan Haughlin—the clan of Gnomes that all Halflings belong to.

Then the parents bid their brood go and fetch the fermals. Mr. and Mrs. Boulger went about the room, snuffing the paper lanterns in the windows until only the light of the fire remained. When the room was dark and the children were gathered again, young Jebby was prompted to step forward.

"Uh, this is my fermal, Benji." The boy held up a doll of rags and straw. "Uh... um..."

"Say the words!" Polla whispered from the crowd.

Jebby nodded and dutifully recited the rest of the invocation. "Benji was not here yesterday. He will not be here tomorrow. Just as we were not here once, and we will not be here again someday. We are thankful for the time we had with him. And we shall remember him. Uh…"

"Go on, then," urged his mother.

With a deep breath and a stifled sob, Jebby through the doll into the fire. The flames grew to a cheery roar around the fermal.

"Good gods, this holiday has some bleak traditions," said Goldson, staring into the blaze.

"One wonders why good folk are maligned for not taking part in these barbaric rituals," agreed Baggs.

One by one, the other children gave similarly reluctant recitals, each naming their fermal before giving it over to the hungry fire. They all looked sad to do it, and the tiniest of them began to cry. Her tears were short-lived, however, as Mr. Boulger was quick to make an announcement once the last fermal was burning.

"Well done, children! And now it's time for presents!" Freddy cried.

"I thought the fermals were the presents," Goldson said to Baggs.

"Oh, there's a silly new habit among the young." Mr. Baggs was not enough of a traditionalist to participate in any Mordo Ogg's Day rituals, but was too much of one to forego complaining when the customs changed. "Some parents give extra gifts after the fermals nowadays. Apparently they think that crying children goes against the spirit of the day."

"Does it?" Goldson turned to the Ghost of Mordo Ogg's Day Present.

The spirit of the day shrugged. "It makes them happy."

"For what that's worth," said Goldson, watching the dancing children. His face was set in a familiar scowl, but a bright grin spread over it as Jebby opened his gift. It was a wooden man with long, blonde hair and armor shining with golden paint.

"A Johan the Champion doll!" exclaimed the boy. He pressed a little lever cleverly designed to look like the paladin's cloak, and the arm swung a sword. "Oh, thank you mum!"

"And I got a Power Broker Barbialleitha!" cried a Halfling girl, holding up a doll fashioned to look like a pretty Elf with a sharp suit and an impossibly small waist.

"An Imperial carriage! With a Mud Drake to pull it!"

"A Flicker Spaniel stuffy! Oh, come here, doggie!"

The children laughed and leapt up and down as they announced their new toys, and the phantasmal voyeurs watching them were nearly as delighted.

"Baggs! All of those were manufactured by the Knight Brothers Toy Company!" exclaimed Goldson.

"Yes," said the ghost. "What of it?"

"Knight Brothers is a wholly owned subsidiary of the Goldson Baggs Group! Ha!" Mr. Goldson danced a hobbling jig of his own. "You know Baggs, I quite like this new tradition."

"We shall have to talk to the lads in marketing down at Knight Brothers shortly," said the Halfling. "Why, with proper advertising, think of the sales if this caught on!"

"We'll have posters up and down the Broad Steps," said Goldson. "Billboards from the Base to Pinnacle Plaza."

"Maybe a mascot to deliver the toys?" suggested Baggs. "Someone the bards can sing songs about on street corners. We'll say he brings the toys for the children."

"Perhaps. The marketers can sort it out," said Goldson with an indifferent shrug. "The point is that everybody should know that giving children toys is a Mordo Ogg's Day tradition. It's as important as lanterns and fireworks."

"More important." Baggs winked.

"No!" bellowed the ghost.

Baggs and Goldson froze, and then looked up at the ghost with renewed consternation. "Ah, right. You're still here," said the Halfling.

The ghost looked incensed in a cantankerous way that reminded Goldson of himself. Deep wrinkles were carving themselves into the spirit's old face. "This is not what Mordo Ogg's Day is for! It is not for more business, more profits, more money!"

"It's beginning to sound rather pointless again," grumbled Goldson.

"It is about sharing joy and happiness with all mankind, and most of all, with those you love!" cried the spirit. "It is a time to—"

"Buy! Buy! Buy!"

Goldson looked at the children. Whatever game they were playing, Barbialleitha had taken charge. The young Halfling walked the stiff-legged Elf doll past the other toys, making demands of all of them.

"I want all the stock in your carriage now! Buy it!" demanded Barbialleitha.

"Yes, ma'am!" said the toy Mud Drake.

"Please don't take my house," begged Jebby's toy paladin.

There was no mercy in Barbialleitha's wooden eyes. "Well you shouldn't have bought it if you can't pay the mortgage!"

"Remind me to keep an eye on that girl," Baggs whispered to Goldson.

Barbialleitha's financial rampage likely would have continued had Freddy not intervened. "Children, there will be plenty of time for playing tomorrow! But now, look! Evening is falling. Do you know what that means?"

"Fireworks!" chorused the children.

"Do we own a fireworks company?" Goldson asked Baggs as the Boulger family and company bundled up in heavy jackets and scarves.

"We might," said Baggs.

"We should. Let's investigate come morning."

"Are you so determined to learn nothing from this?" wheezed the Ghost of Mordo Ogg's Day Present. The spirit was still tall, but stooped now, and not just from the Halflings' low ceiling. His hair was more silver than not. "Do you truly still believe this is just another day? Are your old hearts so fossilized that you are completely closed to any possibility of joy?"

"We are quite open to joy, provided it arrives alongside good sense and profit," said Baggs.

"Show us whatever mummer's farce you wish. It cannot change the fact that we have no time for the little triflings of your holiday," said Goldson.

"If you will not consider the condition of mortals, then perhaps you will ponder the infinite," said the ghost. "Come."

He led them out the door and onto the streets, which were already crowded with eager onlookers. A few street lamps burned at the insistence of the bannermen, but all of the paper lanterns had been doused. All eyes were focused upward, watching in eager anticipation.

A loud pop and a slash of glowing orange and green across the sky heralded the start of the fireworks display. The crowds below gasped appreciatively before bursting into choruses of their favorite Mordo Ogg's Day songs.

"The fireworks draw people's eyes to the stars," said the Ghost of Mordo Ogg's Day Present. He was an elderly man now, as bent and gray as his mortal wards. "And when the lights fade, they stare into the endless space beyond them, and remember that they too will flicker out."

Goldson stared into the purplish void, filled with innumerable pinpricks of light. "Magnificent," he breathed, just before a resounding boom brought a splash of crimson across the horizon.

"It is this realization, this certainty, that binds all mortals. Everyone will die. Everyone must make the most of what they have. And most of them have this day to recognize that they share a common fate, and so on this day they share more of their time and treasure with their fellow man," intoned the ghost.

Goldson nodded mutely, but than a thought struck him. "Most?" he asked.

"Most," confirmed the ghost in a whisper. "But not all."

The Dwarf turned to confront the giant, but the spirit was gone, along with the street and Freddy and all of the crowd. Now he and Baggs were in a sparsely furnished room next to a great picture window. Goldson recognized it as the accounting office on the fifth floor of the main Goldson Baggs building, mostly because of one figure sitting miserably at a desk next to them.

Brock Ratchet had no more tears to cry as he sat working on the quarterly reports, but he still flinched whenever one of the fireworks burst outside.

"It seems the reports needed more attention than expected," said Baggs. "Perhaps it's good he gave them the extra effort."

"Perhaps." An unwelcome thought flew into Goldson's mind, and he had no way to loose it except to give it voice. "But… but what of little Lance?"

"I am sure he will be fine," said Baggs, but his voice held no certainty.

"Will he, spirit?" asked Goldson. "Will the child forgive his father? Will he really be all right?"

The Ghost of Mordo Ogg's Day Present did not answer. When Goldson looked for him, he saw only a heavy fog, rolling in as though it were a chill day on the riverfront. He turned back, and Brock was gone as well, along with the accounting office. "Baggs!" he cried.

"I am here," Baggs called from nearby. "Where are you?"

With a couple more shouts, they came within sight of one another. "Do you suppose the vision of Mordo Ogg's Day Present is over?" Goldson asked his partner.

"I do," said Baggs. "But I cannot say the same for our ordeal."

Goldson nodded. "Then that makes this—"

"Yes, our third haunting." Baggs pointed through the mists, where a great figure in a black hood and robes was approaching them.

STAVE IV:

THE LAST OF THE SPIRITS

The phantom bore down upon them with slow purpose. Its robes flapped in a wind that Goldson could not feel, and it stared into his soul with eyes he could not see. Nothing was visible in the endless night of that dark hood. Bells were playing somewhere in the fog to the tune of "A Song of Three Spirits," and the voice of little Lance singing the words creeped into the old Dwarf's mind.

The third ghost is what's yet to be,
A silent shade unbending.
For the part of life no man can see
Is the bit after the ending.

The spirit was upon them now, looming like a tall ship in the mists.

"You are the Ghost of Mordo Ogg's Day Yet to Come, I presume?" Mr. Baggs asked.

The ghost did not reply. It only pointed to something in the fog beyond the businessmen. When they turned to see what the specter beckoned to, the gloom had parted to reveal a cobbled street, on the fifth or sixth tier perhaps, and on the sidewalk two people were engaged in a conversation.

Goldson and Baggs exchanged a stern look and a nod, and then turned to the vision.

"And a good day it is!" said the shorter of the people. It was Brother Dorgenson, from the Temple of Oppo. "It seems one of our favorite trees is about to bear long due fruit."

"On Mordo Ogg's Day, no less!" said the second, a young Human in a smart suit. She looked familiar to Goldson.

"Of course! What better way to celebrate the season than by aiding the poor?" said Brother Dorgenson.

"And you'll not find a better day for sticking a poker in the eye of the big banks! Or at least one in particular," snickered the woman.

"What's that now?" asked Goldson.

Brother Dorgenson smiled, but he shook his head. "No, no, Miss Ratchet. It's not for revenge or bitterness that we've lobbied His Majesty so. There is no one else to give the poor the help they need, and so I must implore upon the king for action."

A cold fear further chilled the depths of Goldson's heart. "Spirit! What is this nonsense they're on about?"

"Bones! That's Marta Ratchet!" gasped Baggs.

Goldson startled, but saw that it was true. Brock Ratchet's eldest daughter had shed all vestiges of childhood, and now she looked like a young professional at the threshold of a most obnoxious career.

"This is only the first step," Marta was saying to Brother Dorgenson. "We need greater transparency and accountability on the Wall! And then a better system of fairly distributing the yields of our labors."

"May Oppo see it so," said the priest. "But even if not, today shall mark a monumental step when the king signs your petition into law. It must fill you with pride to have played such a role in the civic advancement of our kingdom."

"What law?" Baggs wore the face of an adventurer about to open a suspiciously well-dusted casket in an otherwise dingy crypt. "Spirit, what law will the king sign?"

The ghost said nothing.

"Pride doesn't drive me at my work," said Miss Ratchet. "Nor revenge, though a touch of retribution for that wretched company does much to make my burdens feel lighter. All my labor is for my brother. My prayers are that he will notice my efforts, wherever he is, and know of my love."

"Does she mean little Lance?" Goldson asked.

"What law was she speaking of?" demanded Baggs.

But the Ghost of Mordo Ogg's Day Yet to Come remained silent. It raised its hand, draped in black robes, to point at something else. Marta and Brother Dorgenson faded into the fog, and when the mists parted again they were in the Ratchets' living room once more.

It was different now. The scavenged furnishings seemed duller in hue, and the lanterns cast less light. Mrs. Ratchet worked in the kitchen, attended by two of her children, nearly grown. Her movements were slower, less jubilant, than they had been when Goldson had last seen her, and it was more than age that weighed her down.

The door opened, and Brock Ratchet entered, carrying a pair of pigeons on a string. "Hello, dear ones," he said. "There'll be meat for the pie today!"

"Well done, Mr. Ratchet!" said his wife. "What a clever snare you set, catching two birds. I hope everyone is hungry."

"I will eat," said Mr. Ratchet. The misery behind his smile was revealed as it faded, like rocks under melting snow. "That will have to do. I can muster no joy this time of year."

Mrs. Ratchet nodded and shot him her own brave smile before she set back to work.

"But what became of their happiness? Their good cheer of years gone?" Goldson asked the ghost.

The ghost stared down at him, its gaze as black and empty as infinity.

"Ghost! What... what became of little Lance?" Goldson asked again.

The spirit pointed to the fireplace. Goldson turned to find a small chair set inside a circle of salt next to the embers. A child's crutch was set atop it, along with a tiny wreath of flowers and holly and a woodcut of little Lance.

"Ah," sighed Goldson sadly. "The boy did not make it. I am sorry to see as much."

"A pity," agreed Baggs, inclining his head. And then, after the smallest pause that decorum demanded, "Spirit, what law did Marta Ratchet and Brother Dorgenson speak of?"

"Indeed, it sounded rather dire," said Goldson.

There was a knock at the door, and when Brock answered it he was embraced by Marta.

"Ah, good. There she is now," said Baggs.

"Hush. I want to hear what she says," said Goldson.

The Ghost of Mordo Ogg's Day Yet to Come seemed taken aback. It pointed again at the shrine of the empty chair and crutch, waving its robed hand with more emphasis.

"What?" asked Baggs. "Oh, yes. Yes, it is very sad."

"Truly tragic," said Goldson, and he meant it. "The child seemed like a good boy, and it was unfortunate to see him meet his fate so early. And yet, ghosts have no business in the mortal realms—"

"No offense to present company," said Baggs.

"—while the living have a lot of work to attend to," finished Goldson.

"Such as that law that Marta spoke of," added Baggs. "And may speak of again, if we're lucky. Let's watch."

"Yes, let's," said Goldson. He and Baggs settled in to watch the Ratchets with keen eyes.

The Ghost of Mordo Ogg's Day Yet to Come reached an arm into its hood in a manner that suggested rubbing spectral temples. It waved its other hand at the businessmen in exasperation.

"What?" asked Goldson. "Are you still on about the boy? We must accept the poor child's fate and move on. What's done is done."

The ghost held its arms above its head and waved.

Baggs sighed. "Well, yes, we know it hasn't happened yet, technically. But it surely will happen, and there is nothing to be done about it."

That seemed to incense the spirit even more. It loomed and pointed at the pair ominously.

"I beg your pardon," demanded Goldson. "Are you implying this is our doing?"

"What could we have possibly done to change the boy's fate?" scoffed Baggs.

The ghost turned back to Brock, who was still holding his daughter.

"There, there," said Marta. "Mrs. Creegan says that he will see justice. We have a strong case."

An errant tear trickled down Mr. Ratchet's face. "No amount of justice will bring my boy back! If only I had spent more time with my little Lance," he choked.

"It wasn't your fault," said Marta. "If those horrible bosses of yours at Goldson Baggs had let you take the time for your family, you could have!"

"And if their healing plan had covered his condition, our little Lance never would have been pulled into the netherworld," added Mrs. Ratchet.

"Or even if they'd paid a decent enough wage that you could pay for the care yourself," piped up one of the children.

"Then again, if they'd invested more heavily in healing magic and the restorative arts, a cure for Lance could have been more readily available and cheaper," said Marta.

Mrs. Ratchet snorted. "Invested? By the gods, if Goldson Baggs only ran the healers and apothecaries they own without taking a profit, we might have afforded his treatment on our own."

"As we could have if business leaders like Mr. Goldson and Mr. Baggs endorsed fiscal policies that support a strong middle class," finished Marta.

The Ghost of Mordo Ogg's Day Yet to Come looked back at the ancient Dwarf and Halfling. The empty darkness beneath its hood radiated smugness.

"You really have no idea how things work, do you?" said Goldson.

"Our investors have not put us in place to run charitable endeavors," said Baggs. "Whether you like it or not, the markets demand performance, and performance demands focus on the bottom line."

"If we did all of that nonsense the Ratchets described, you can be sure the board of investors would merely replace us with sufficiently hardened executives," said Goldson.

"I certainly would vote to do as much to any soft-hearted leaders at the companies I invest in," added Baggs.

"It is how markets work. It is the way of the world," Goldson told the ghost.

Mr. Baggs nodded sagely. "You may detest the nature of the game, but you should not hate its players."

"It is not our responsibility, nor our fault," said Goldson.

They stared up at the ghost, jaws locked and faces screwed up in defiance. The ghost stared back, though it was unclear if it was in confusion or consternation. Eventually, the spirit's head tilted in a way reminiscent of an exaggerated eye roll, and it stepped away. Thick mists flowed into the room behind the phantom, and soon Goldson and Baggs were enveloped in fog with no choice but to follow the ghost.

When the spectral vapors parted once more, they were in a mahogany office with a conference table in the center. Four high back chairs ringed the table, and from their vantage point Goldson and Baggs could see three figures in fine suits seated around it.

The tallest of them sat as though she had been neatly folded and placed into her chair. A nameplate next to her said "MRS. CREEGAN" in polished brass letters. "I think it likely the king's arbiter will refer this case to a jury of nobles," she said.

"So much the better," said a Dwarf with a long, golden beard. A plaque by his side identified him as Mr. Jerrakson. "The tale of little Lance Ratchet in particular will sway the jury most convincingly. With the Ratchet's joining the class action, his story shall be front and center in the courtroom."

"Good gods, Baggs! We're being sued!" cried Goldson, a sudden terror gripping him.

"The poor boy's fate has already swayed the court of public opinion," said a Scribkin named Mrs. Noufangled. "As has the defendants' onerous behavior regarding the holiday. Did you know they repeatedly forced non-essential employees to work on Mordo Ogg's Day?"

"I heard they never decorated their offices for the holiday," said Mr. Jerrakson.

"A nice touch," said Mrs. Creegan. "But the real indictment of their character is that we have sworn affidavits from officials at several charities claiming that they were personally rebuffed by Mr. Goldson and Mr. Baggs with special malice on Mordo Ogg's Day."

"Hearsay and rumors!" snarled Mr. Baggs. "Our lawyers will run this scurrilous case from the courts!"

"And what does our newest partner have to offer?" asked Mrs. Noufangled.

"Surely you must be happier to be on this side of the case," said Mr. Jerrakson, grinning.

They all turned to the chair with its back to Goldson and Baggs, whose jaws dropped in unison as the seat's occupant leaned forward and spoke.

"Well, of course I must recuse myself from the matter officially," said Fredegar Boulger. "But I can provide character witnesses that will sign sworn testimony that Bolbi Baggs does not celebrate any holidays with his family, let alone Mordo Ogg's Day."

"Who would wish to spend time with such backstabbing, traitorous Goblin-snots?" shrieked Baggs.

"Good," said Mrs. Creegan. "The more we can do to make Mr. Goldson and Mr. Baggs appear heartless and cruel, the better our case against them."

"Making those two appear wicked is an easy task," laughed Mrs. Noufangled.

"All the more so for their particular malice toward the holidays," said Mr. Jerrakson. "Just as the season shines a particularly strong light on charitable acts, it also sets those who are unkind or uncharitable on a pedestal for public scorn."

"I agree that highlighting the deficiency of character in my uncle and his partner is a sound strategy," said Freddy. "But that alone cannot be the basis of our case."

"Indeed it cannot." A measure of confidence returned to Goldson.

"Which is why I can discreetly recommend that the clerks working on the case look into a few settlements that the Goldson Baggs Group made during my tenure there," said Freddy with a devious smile. "And a clever investigator might inquire about how they came by that contract up in Bloodroot that made them a fortune last year."

"You wretch!" Baggs's round face had turned more crimson than the holly berries on the windowsill. He leapt at his nephew, but Freddy was already fading away. The mists closed around the lawyers' office, and the quartet was gone, leaving nothing but a trace of laughter hanging in the air.

"Spirit! Tell me they do not win!" pleaded Goldson. "Tell me that the jurors see reason!"

The silent phantom only pointed to a black door rising in the mists.

"What—what is that?" asked Baggs.

As Goldson and Baggs stared, the ebony portal swung inward. Beyond it lay a familiar sight, though with some differences. The curtains had changed. There was a new chair by each desk. A small marble bust of an Orc was set near the window. But otherwise, it was the personal office of Mr. Goldson and Mr. Baggs, just as Goldson had left it the afternoon before.

The room was occupied by their future selves. Future Goldson and Future Baggs didn't look older for the intervening time, but then again, it would have been very difficult for any recent version of Goldson or Baggs to look much older than they already did. Yet, there was some distinction: the vision of Goldson Yet to Come looked very weary and far more angry than his prior self. And now that they stared at the faces of their future, the earlier Goldson and Baggs looked less substantial, almost spectral. Goldson felt as though they were fading into memory.

"Five hundred million giltin?" he shouted. "You think those devils will get a king's ransom for this slander?"

A Human clerk stood at ground zero of the businessmen's wrath. "It's, uh, it's actually a rather conservative estimate," he ventured.

"Five hundred million?" said the prior Baggs, staring into space.

His future self was much more animated. "Conservative? You mean to tell me you think these charlatans could take more? Have you no defense against this frivolous lawsuit?"

"These peasants are taking us to court for not being festive enough, and our lawyers can do nothing about it!" scoffed future Goldson.

"Uh, your pardons, sirs." The clerk cleared his throat. "But you're actually being taken to court for the cuts you made to the company healing plan and the subsequent rise in mortality rates among—"

"We saw court filings about Mordo Ogg's Day decorations!" snarled Baggs Yet to Come. "Lawyers are actually arguing about holly sprigs and lantern placements!"

"Sir, those filings by the plaintiffs are meant to show the nature of your character. Er, your alleged character," the clerk quickly corrected. "It's a good strategy to win a jury; people judge each other much more harshly this time of year."

"What happened to giving goodwill toward all of mankind?" snorted Goldson.

"I think giving goodwill toward adherents of similar traditions is far more common, sir," said the clerk.

Future Baggs huffed and looked back at his ledger. "But five hundred million? Good gods, that's more money than some city-states have in their coffers!"

"Now we've no margin for error if we're to make our numbers in the fourth quarter," grumbled Goldson. "And it technically has yet to start!"

"We'll miss the projections!" gasped the specter of Goldson.

"Spirit! Show us no more!" cried Baggs. "Tell us how we may avoid this calamity!"

The clerk shuffled his papers and cleared his throat with a wince. "There is, uh, other news, sirs. From the palace."

"Are you still here?" Baggs asked, already working at his ledger once more.

"Well, I didn't want to be the one to tell you," said the wavering clerk. "I really, truly didn't. But I drew the short straw to discuss the healing plan lawsuit with you, and the team said only one of us should have their Mordo Ogg's Day ruined..."

The phantoms of Goldson and Baggs grew even more pale. "Spirit, is this the law of which Brother Dorgenson and Marta spoke?" Goldson asked.

The phantom was as cold and silent as the grave.

"It's just that the trial has made a lot of unpleasant things public." Sweat was beading on the babbling clerk like morning dew. "The story of little Lance, the other casualties, the... the lack of Mordo Ogg's Day spirit..."

"What sort of law is it?" asked the specter of Baggs, his face filled with dread. "Spirit! What law is it?"

"All of it has swayed the opinion of the masses against the firm significantly. Not that our image was terribly positive to begin with," said the clerk. "And now the king is eager to show the people that he is on their side of the matter. It's about public relations, really."

"Bones!" swore Baggs Yet to Come.

"Get to the point, man!" barked future Goldson.

"It's more taxes and regulations, sir," squeaked the man. He held up a printed notice from the King of Andarun. It bore an announcement of the new tax rates above a woodcut of the royal crest. "The King signed a ten percent hike on corporate earnings not an hour ago, along with aggressive standards of care for company healing plans. Effective today."

"We'll lose tens of billions!" shrieked future Baggs.

"We'll miss all of our annual projections!" cried his partner.

"Nooo—!" howled the specter of Baggs, dropping to his knees.

"Spirit! Please! One more chance!" Goldson grasped the robes of the Ghost of Mordo Ogg's Day Yet to Come. "I beg of you, give us one more chance to change this horrible fate! One more chance! We'll change! We'll change!"

Goldson pressed his face into the robes as he pleaded, but as his tearful appeal continued he became aware that his beard was no longer scratching against the burlap robes of the wraith, but instead sliding against his smooth silk sheets, fresh and free of any sausage grease.

TAX

" —Nooo!" Baggs finished, still thrashing in the bed next to Goldson's.

Mr. Goldson sat up. The sun had yet to crest above the Wall, but the blue glow of twilight hung in the air, and he could see the room was undisturbed down to the myriad holy symbols hanging from every furnishing. "It's morning!" he hollered. "Baggs! Wake up! It's Mordo Ogg's Day morning!"

STAVE V:

THE END OF IT

"Come *on,* hurry!" Goldson leapt from his bed as fast as his creaking bones would move. "We can fix it all if we hurry, Baggs!"

"Eh? What day is it?" Mr. Baggs sat up with his nightcap skewed and draped over one eye.

"It's Mordo Ogg's Day, of course!" Goldson nodded at the icon of Dakran hanging from his bed post. "Look! All is as it was last night! Come! I have a plan to fix all the ills we witnessed!"

"A plan? Already?" Baggs shook his head.

"To fix all ills!" shouted Goldson. "But only if we hurry!"

He explained the scheme to Baggs as they rushed to dress themselves—or perhaps half-dress themselves, for Goldson's shirt was wide open and Baggs still wore his nightcap as they charged down the stairs. The Dwarf hurried to throw the drapes open, and through the big shop front windows he could see the shadows receding as dawn's light spilled over the Wall.

The morning glow spilled into the room, illuminating the arcane devices and vials set out across the tables and desks. Mirnen MacLeod and Avalon Tarunin huddled behind one such device as though it were a shield, and gave cautious salutations once it was apparent that Goldson and Baggs saw them.

"Aha, good morning, sirs," stuttered the cleric. "I'm afraid our results were—"

"Not now! Never mind that now!" Goldson said. "Tell me, cleric, who is the most skilled healer in your temple?"

"Uh—that would be High Priestess Pellathana," said MacLeod. "Her Holiness has been favored by Musana for a thousand years, and the wisdom of—"

"Fine, good," said Goldson. "We wish to hire her. Have Her Holiness meet us on the Broad Steps down by the… Baggs, what tier did the Ratchets live on?"

Panic and confusion vied for control of the cleric's face. "Uh, sirs—" she started.

Baggs shrugged. "Gods if I know. Down at the base, if the decor was any indication."

"Have her meet us by Fafnir's Gate on the second tier in two hours," Goldson told the cleric. "She must bring whatever she needs for occult matters as well; I suspect it's to be an exorcism as much as a healing."

"But sirs!" protested MacLeod. "It is Mordo Ogg's Day! Her Holiness will be holding services in the temple all morning."

"So it is! It's Mordo Ogg's Day!" said Goldson, raising a smile like a buckler. And then, tentatively, like a warrior trying out a new sword of uncertain enchantment, he added, "Good cheer to you."

"Happy Mordo Ogg's Day!" said Baggs. "And please know that while we totally respect the spirit of the season—"

"Completely," interjected Goldson.

"—we do have a matter of charity that is of the utmost importance, and the High Priestess's compensation shall reflect that. Shall we say ten thousand giltin as a personal fee to Her Holiness?" A wide smile wrinkled Baggs's leathery face.

"And another ten thousand donated to the temple?" Goldson nodded encouragingly.

"No sirs. No amount... am.... amount... ahm... um... I... ah..." The cleric's brain had apparently finally processed the businessmen's offer, and was so taxed by the enormity of the sums that she needed another moment to figure out how to redirect the sentence. "Ahem. No amount of festivity should keep the Temple of Musana from a healer's duty. I shall tell High Priestess Pellathana of your need."

"Good!" said Goldson. "Off you go, then! And you! Wizard!"

"Sir?" Tarunin had looked considerably more attentive and hopeful once Goldson and Baggs began throwing promises of gold about.

"We need your help. Is that strong-looking Elf still standing guard out there?"

The noctomancer glanced out the window. "Zeerith? Yes, he—"

"Good! Have a servant ready the carriage, and then you both ride with us!"

"We'll pay you all double time for the holiday," added Baggs. "Make sure you mention as much."

The wizard looked at the apparatus on the table, shrugged, and scurried out to make the necessary preparations. The carriage was waiting for Goldson and Baggs out front by the time they finished neatening up their clothes and finalizing their plans. Zeerith and Avalon saw the old men into the coach before hopping onto the jump seat. Goldson shouted hurried instructions to the driver, shut the door, and they were away.

First was a trip up to the tenth tier, where a dusting of snow was blowing in from the heights of Mount Wynspar. The white powder swirled amidst the glowing paper lanterns lit along every street. Mordo Ogg's candles shone in the windows, and the most devout citizens were already headed off to the temples.

Goldson stared out the window at the masses. "The challenge will be how to speak to people," he confided to Baggs. "Small talk with Arth's elite is easy enough, but it's been ages since I've entertained a conversation with the common man for more than five minutes without assigning him a task or firing him."

"Don't worry," Baggs assured him. "The mechanics of the traditions are easy to grasp. Why, just a few expressions represent half of the requisite holiday spirit. A word of 'happy Mordo Ogg's Day,' or 'peace on Arth, goodwill toward Man,' or the supremely inane observation that 'it's the season' will be welcomed by all, almost regardless of context, and credited to the speaker as an appropriate amount of cheer."

"Surely there must to be more nuance to it than that!" said Goldson.

Baggs smiled and shook his head. "Not so much as you'd imagine. These holiday invocations can be used under almost any circumstances around this time of year. 'Gods bless us,' is especially useful."

"What? For when we all sneeze?" scoffed Goldson.

"Ha! Surely, but with the proper inflection it could be anything from a wish against ill will to an expression of joy. Just make an effort to tag some such festive clause to the end of every other sentence you utter, and the people who hear you will be all the happier for it."

"It all seems like hogwash to me," muttered Goldson.

"It's the season for it," said Baggs with a smirk.

Their driver urged the horses on at reckless speed as they rode up to the main office of the Goldson Baggs Group Incorporated. Goldson drafted a quick memo enacting a couple of policy changes. Baggs tasked a pair of assistants with delivering the notice and additional instructions to several key employees. Then they were off again, careening across the snow-dusted cobblestones as fast as the beleaguered horses could run.

They called for more stops along the way down the mountain. A baker on the eighth tier was open, hoping to sell tea cakes and fruit breads to ill-prepared parents. Mr. Baggs made all of her wildest dreams come true, and soon the carriage smelled of cinnamon and currants and fresh-baked bread.

Other vendors were less enterprising. A toy seller on the sixth tier was roused from slumber by Goldson banging on his door. It took the shouts of the entire carriage to rouse the butcher across the square. A tailor at the end of the street didn't wake until Baggs commanded the noctomancer to blow the doors off the tailor's shop with a conjured bolt of lightning. The intrusions were met with varying degrees of surprise and anger, but no objection was so great that it couldn't be papered over with a large bank cheque. Goldson and Baggs left all of the merchants feeling far more jolly than they found them.

They left the upper tiers then, racing down the cart lane of the Broad Steps so fast that Goldson surmised they had been cut loose from the horses and were careening unhindered down the mountain. The idea was thrown from his head when the carriage jerked roughly and turned off the steps.

"Where are we?" yelled Goldson, gripping the handrail.

"Second tier! Near Dunedling Fens, by the look of it!" shouted Baggs, his face pressed against the carriage window. "There's our man!"

The carriage lurched to a stop, and an attendant from the street rushed up to speak with the driver. A few moments later, a clerk opened the door and invited Goldson and Baggs to follow her.

She led them down a side alley off the main street, followed by Zeerith and Tarunin. The warrior carried several large parcels, and the wizard walked in front of a train of several more packages that bobbed through the air on sorcerous currents. They hadn't gone far when they saw Brother Dorgenson speaking with a grizzled-looking Human in a town crier's hat.

The Dwarven priest seemed annoyed when he noticed the clerk returning. "As I said, I'm in the middle of an interview at the moment—" he began, but his tone changed quickly when he noticed two of the richest men on Arth hurrying behind her. "Mr. Goldson! Mr. Baggs! Uh, to what do I—?"

"Brother Dorgenson!" said Baggs, shaking the priest's hand warmly. "A happy Mordo Ogg's Day to you!"

"Uh, yes. Thank you. And, er, a happy Mordo Ogg's Day to you," said Dorgenson, looking more confused than convivial. "But, uh, last night you said…"

"Oh, never mind that! Never mind!" said Goldson. "Don't begrudge old men their ill-humor at a late hour. We're afflicted with arthritis and indigestion as the day wanes."

"But this blessed morning finds us in good spirits," said Baggs. "Look! We've brought gifts and supplies for your poor charges." On his cue, Zeerith and Tarunin opened up their packages to reveal bundles of warm clothes, thick blankets, and smoked meats.

"I… I don't know what to say." Brother Dorgenson looked in awe at the bounty before him. "I… I cannot find words!"

The town crier next to him located a few. "And you're donating all of this to the poor?" he pressed.

"Of course!" said Baggs. "Alongside a donation of ten thousand giltin to charities run by the Temple of Oppo for their work with the poor."

"Ten thousand?" squeaked Brother Dorgenson.

The town crier licked his lips and set his charcoal pencil against his notepad. "Would you care to make a statement to the Order of Town Criers regarding this generous gift?"

Goldson shot Baggs a sidelong grin.

"Oh, we would," said the old Dwarf. "Very much so. But unfortunately, we must rush to present another Mordo Ogg's Day gift."

"Some might say an even more spectacularly generous one," added Baggs.

So it was that when Goldson and Baggs left Brother Dorgenson stunned amidst the piles of goods and presents, the town crier came running at their heels. The Human's pencil scrabbled furiously on his notepad as they clambered into the black coach. The carriage sagged as the wizard and warrior hopped into the jump seat. Then the driver cracked his reins, and they were off once more.

The palanquin of High Priestess Pellathana was waiting for them at Fafnir's Gate, attended by Mirnen Macleod. It was a white tent decorated with golden sunbursts and held aloft by four gilded golems that fell into step behind the black carriage. Clerks in dark suits, riding horses and bearing the parcels Goldson and Baggs had ordered, rode alongside the high priestess as the procession advanced. Looking back at the holy litter and the riders flanking it, Goldson felt as though he was riding at the crest of a great wave sloshing Ridgeward through Sculpin Downs.

At the direction of a clerk sent in advance, the generous tide crashed against a ramshackle building in a derelict corner of the second tier. It was a warren of apartments, built in the style of Halflings with all the doors facing frontward and connected by a teetering network of porches and stairs. Chimneys stuck out from the sides of the building at odd angles, sending thin streams of smoke trickling into the clouds.

Goldson and Baggs shouted commands as they climbed down from their carriage. MacLeod and a pair of paladins in bright armor tried to secure a place for the High Priestess to disembark. Clerks and attendants rushed to unload the carriage and calm the horses. Onlookers began to gather, curious about the strange procession.

The commotion was enough to attract the attention of several of the tenants of the warren. Several surprised residents opened their doors, but none of them were more shocked than Mr. Brock Ratchet when he stepped out of apartment three.

"Mr. Goldson?" said the surprised accountant. "And Mr. Baggs!"

"Happy Mordo Ogg's Day!" said Mr. Goldson. "A glad day to you all!"

"We hope you'll forgive the intrusion," added Mr. Baggs. "But we became aware of an anomaly with the healing plan that must be remedied."

"And what better day for making things right than this blessed holiday?" said Goldson.

Mrs. Ratchet peeked out of the door from behind her husband, and though she didn't recognize either of the renowned businessmen on her doorstep, she gasped at the burden of the warrior behind them. "Is that a griffin haunch?"

"The finest the butcher had," said Baggs. "We hoped to join you for Mordo Ogg's Day morning tea, and planned to make recompense by bringing your dinner."

"If it's not too much trouble." Goldson smiled.

The Ratchets needed a moment to recover from the shock, but they quickly bade the guests enter their apartment. Brock led Mr. Goldson and Mr. Baggs to the couch, apologizing profusely for the state of their living room. Marta and Peta were already seated there, and they smiled wanly as the rest of the procession entered. There was only room for the high priestess, the paladins, and the town crier. And the griffin haunch, of course; Mrs. Ratchet muttered and fussed about spices and cooking times as she hauled the massive cut to the kitchen.

They were still settling in when a wooden clatter startled Goldson. Little Lance stood at the doorway to the back room, his crutch fallen beside him. The boy stared at the High Priestess of Musana and let out an inhuman snarl. A sickening light bloomed in the skull-shaped birthmark on his brow.

"I presume this boy is the one to be healed," said High Priestess Pellathana. The silver-haired Elf pulled a flask and several small scrolls from her long white and gold robes. "I will need—"

"Save your naive mewlings, servant of the callow gods!" boomed little Lance in a voice like thunder. A sickly, greenish luminescence erupted from his eyes and mouth, and the sinister glow around him took the form of waving tentacles. With an inhuman roar, the boy sent a blast of viridescent fire rolling toward the high priest, setting many of the Mordo Ogg's Day decorations alight in the process. One of the paladins of Musana stepped forward and conjured a shield of golden light to block the unholy flames.

Mrs. Ratchet shrieked and dove behind the stove. Mr. Ratchet hollered and grabbed a poker from the fireplace. Goldson and Baggs hunkered behind a dilapidated couch.

Lance threw more fire, hurled obscenities, and struck at the clergy with his waving tentacles. The high priestess ignored the occult assault, protected as she was by the holy magics of the paladins in front of her. The Elf strode forward with grim purpose and murmured chants, brandishing her scrolls like weapons.

"Thrice curse you! Back, fleshling! I shall lick the marrow from your bones at the end of all things!" Despite his threats, Lance scrabbled back like a cornered animal. *"Gods curse you, every one!"* he shrieked at the assembled guests before he fled into the dark of the back room.

"After him!" shouted High Priestess Pellathana. The holy woman strode into the bedchambers after the ensorcelled boy, flanked by her paladins.

Brock Ratchet turned back to his employers, who were stamping out bits of burning holly that had fallen too close. "B-but, but what will they—"

"Don't worry," said Mr. Goldson, dusting embers from his coat. "I'm sure—"

The back room erupted with shafts of white-hot light, casting the Ratchet's apartment in stark relief. Goldson staggered back as an animal scream and shouts in an ancient dialect of Elven rang out. The

noise was sustained until all present were covering their ears, and then it cut off as quickly as it had come.

"Good gods," said Baggs, rubbing at his eyes.

"Indeed they are," said the High Priestess. She strode from the back room with the crumpled form of little Lance cradled in her arms. "The boy will live."

"Lance!" cried Mr. and Mrs. Ratchet, and all of their other children. The family rushed to the boy's side. He was even paler than before, and there were deep circles under his eyes, but the birthmark on his forehead had receded until it was little more than a bump of discolored flesh.

"Father," whispered the child. He gave his sire a weak smile.

"The spirit in him will need to be re-bound once a year," the priestess told them as she handed Lance off to Mr. Ratchet. "But provided that he sees a healer annually, he should have a long and happy life."

"How fortunate, then, that our healing plans now cover predestined conditions once more," Mr. Goldson pointed out. "Little Lance will have access to all of the care he needs."

"Provided you remain in our employ, of course," said Mr. Baggs. "Not all companies have such generous healing plans."

"Indeed they do not, sirs!" cried Mr. Ratchet, holding his boy to his chest. "Thank you! Thank you!"

"You're welcome, my boy!" said Baggs. "And a happy Mordo Ogg's Day to all! Good will to everyone!"

"And also tea cakes," said Goldson. "Mr. Tarunin?"

The wizard levitated in a platter of finely decorated confections. The cakes upon it were still warm, and they filled the air with a sweet aroma that mingled with the scents of Mrs. Ratchet's herbal tea. Baggs raised a steaming mug in toast to Lance's good health before everyone fetched a tea cake.

Only Marta's joy was incomplete. She was clearly happy for her brother, and regarded Lance with a radiant smile whenever his gaze turned upon her. Yet she still watched Goldson and Baggs through narrowed eyes when her father's attention was elsewhere. The young woman approached them while her father fetched Lance another tea cake. "Why are you doing this?" she whispered.

"Why, good will toward all men!" tried Mr. Goldson. When her face didn't soften, he added, "It's the season for it, after all."

"No," said Marta. "Good will is universal, but personal visits to deliver tea cakes and expensive healing cannot be achieved at scale. Your proclamations of generosity are loudest and your smiles widest when the town crier is watching, and it's obvious why he traveled here at all."

"Very perceptive of you to notice," said Baggs. "But showing people our festivity does not preclude us from actually being festive."

"Perhaps, but why our family?" said Marta. "There are many families in the city with children as sick as Lance. Some sicker. Why us?"

"It had to be someone," said Goldson. "As you said, we cannot do this at scale. But why kick a fairy for doing a favor? Why not accept good fortune when the gods bring it?"

Marta scowled. "I am not sure it is such good fortune. My father is now bound to remain in your employ if he wishes for my brother to live. He has not had a pay raise in years, but now, how can he press for one when the good health of his son depends on his employers? And what will happen when Lance comes of age, and is not so little anymore? Must he find work at your firm or perish?"

"I..." Goldson's jaw flapped uselessly for a moment. "Peace on Arth?"

Baggs came to his rescue. "I think what Mr. Goldson means is that we must do the good works we can, even if we cannot fix all the world's ills. Though I must say that you're very sharp, asking such questions. I commend your business acumen, Miss

Ratchet." The Halfling pulled a jet-black business card inlaid with gold lettering from his coat pocket. "There's a bright future for you in the private sector, should you want it."

Marta frowned, but she took the card after a moment.

Tea time was otherwise unblemished. The Ratchet family and their surprising guests laughed and told stories around the fire, and toasted Mordo Ogg's Day and Goldson Baggs Incorporated. By the time the cakes were gone and the kettle drained, little Lance was well enough to join in on a Mordo Ogg's Day song. The child's piping voice was higher than all the others as they finished "A Song of Three Spirits."

The man cried, "Where's the third ghost?
For I see only two?"
"Your past and future called tonight,
But the third spirit is you!"

And so the present left his ship
Grateful for the omen.
The past is done, the future dark,
But we live in the moment.

When the songs were done, Goldson, Baggs, and the clergy of Musana made their excuses. Mrs. Ratchet held them tight and planted damp kisses on their cheeks, and little Lance shook both of their hands, and all shouted goodbye as they pulled on their cloaks.

"Oh, and Mr. Ratchet," Goldson mentioned, pausing in the doorway.

"Sir?" Brock turned to Goldson with little Lance perched atop one of his shoulders.

"I do need those reports reviewed by tomorrow."

"Oh." Mr. Ratchet looked up at his son, more vibrant than ever with his birthmark finally subdued. "Of course! Of course, sirs! You've saved my boy! I'll triple-check those reports. I'll work all night if I have to!"

Goldson's grin was the most genuine he'd worn all day. "Gods bless us, every one!" he said, and ducked out the door.

The courtyard outside the apartment was full of people, most of them curious about the wealthy-looking visitors to the Ratchet residence. Goldson and Baggs waved to the onlookers and bid them all a happy Mordo Ogg's Day. Then they said farewell to the high priestess and assured her that a clerk would deliver the bank cheques for her services the very next day. The professional heroes were sent back to work at the fourth tier office, with promises that they would be paid double time for their extra effort. They also parted with the town crier, though only after reiterating the finer points of the gathering to him. Then the old Dwarf and Halfling climbed back into the carriage, and a crack of the whip took them off toward the Broad Steps once more.

"Gods, my face is sore," said Baggs, rubbing at his jaw.

"Mine as well," said Goldson, relieved to wear a comfortable scowl once more. "It's been quite a while since I had to sustain a grin for that long in one stretch."

The respite was short-lived. There was little traffic on the Broad Steps this close to Mordo Ogg's tea, and the ride up to the steps was faster than Goldson would have liked. Too soon they were on the sixth tier, looking at an attractive row of granite townhouses. They stopped by one with a grass and loam facade and a circular oak door popular with some clans of Gnomes, particularly Halflings and Tomte.

Fredegar was rightly surprised when Goldson and Baggs rapped on their door. "Uncle Bolbi!" he exclaimed as he ushered them in. "I thought you could not make it!"

"No, no, my boy. I merely could not accept your invitation at that moment. Not with other people watching," said Baggs.

"We must avoid the appearance of nepotism, you'll recall," said Goldson.

"An easy mistake to make, as you're my closest family," said Baggs. "But away from prying eyes, we can't think of anything more worthwhile than a quiet holiday with your fine family."

"I do hope there's enough food," said Goldson. "We wouldn't want to trouble you."

"No trouble at all!" said Fred. "Come in, come in! Make yourselves at home!"

They did. Baggs positioned himself next to his nephew at the dinner table, where he could most effectively shower the lad with compliments and expressions of affection, peppered with appropriate phrases of holiday spirit. Goldson insisted on sitting next to Otho, and spent the feast plying Lothelia's nephew for information about his aunt's businesses.

Baggs lifted his wineglass after the salad and soup courses, but before the roast griffin had been set upon the table. "I'd like to raise a toast, on this blessed day," he said.

"Hear hear!" said Goldson, raising his own glass. "'Tis the season for it, after all."

The adults around the table raised their own glasses, and the children lifted cups of milk. Young Jebby's mug almost touched the ceiling.

"To family, and friends—"

"And loyalty!" interjected Goldson, nodding to Freddy.

Baggs recovered smoothly, though with a pointed glare at the old Dwarf. "—and love, and all the ties that bind us."

"Gods bless us all!" said Goldson.

"Hear hear!" said the others around the table. They drank, and drank again as Freddy left to fetch a steaming platter of roasted meat.

When the meal was ended and the children had stampeded upstairs, fermals in tow, the adults lolled around the wreckage of the dinner like walruses upon an iceberg. Goldson and Baggs heaped exaggerated compliments upon their hosts, just to be sure the Boulgers were sufficiently inoculated against Otho's virulent subversion.

"Will you stay for a drink and some cards, Uncle?" asked Freddy.

"I'm afraid not, my boy. I hope to see the fireworks from my office," Baggs told him.

"And it's been a long day already for such old men," said Goldson, feigning a pain in his wrist.

"But I must say, I am very glad we came to see you, Nephew," said Baggs.

Freddy beamed, and the smile stayed upon his face until he was waving goodbye to Goldson and Baggs. They returned his jovial expression and waved and called out fond goodbyes as they ascended the steps of their black carriage. The happy facade remained until the coach door shut, and Goldson and Baggs could finally drop the act.

"Ye gods, now I recall why I don't subject myself to those people," said Baggs as the carriage rolled into the street. "I'd almost rather let another firm have him."

"He knows too much," murmured Goldson, setting his ledger upon his lap. "Why, if he worked anywhere else, I'd imagine securing his silence would require you to spend even more time with him and his brood."

"Bones! You're right," said Baggs. "There's no salary I wouldn't pay to avoid that."

"Speaking of expenses," said Goldson, adding some figures. "I'd estimate that we spent a bit over fifty thousand giltin today, including overtime for the servants."

"What about the change to the healing plan?" asked Baggs. "We'll have to cover all predestined conditions now."

Goldson added some numbers and estimates in his head. "A hundred thousand a year on the low end. It could be up to half a million annually, if many more children are afflicted with curses or a big prophecy rolls about."

"So perhaps one or two million in extra expenses over the next five years," said Baggs.

"As good a guess as any," said Goldson. "But now the Ratchets won't join the class action lawsuit, and

Freddy won't help those vultures by betraying our secrets."

"There won't be a lawsuit at all!" laughed Baggs.

"Especially not after all of the wonderful news the town criers will be shouting about us." Goldson sat back in his seat. "And given that the lawsuit would have cost us five hundred million—"

"Not to mention the costs of the tax hike," said Baggs.

"Or the expense of bringing our healing plan in line with excessive regulations," Goldson said.

"I'd say we made quite the handsome return on our investment!" finished Baggs. "Ha! The ghosts of Mordo Ogg's Day have proven most profitable this year."

"Very profitable indeed." Goldson grimaced; he liked the numbers well enough, but the mention of the spirits brought another thought. "Which brings us to less happy news."

"Quite," said Baggs. He readied two small parcels wrapped in checkered cloth—the last of the purchases left in the carriage. "Let's see to it, then."

They rode in sullen silence down to the fourth tier, to the office where they had spent the night before. Dusk was falling, but the lanterns and fire were lit on the first floor, and Goldson could see the silhouettes of the professional heroes through the large windows.

The hired heroes scrambled to tidy up as the door of the carriage opened.

Zeerith of House Illistyneth opened the door for Goldson and Baggs. Mirnen MacLeod greeted the pair as they tromped inside. "Good evening, Mr. Goldson and Mr. Baggs."

Avalon Tarunin wore a hopeful smile. "A Happy Mordo Ogg's Day to you, sirs," he said.

"Is it?" barked Goldson.

"I suppose it might be, depending on what you've caught in these contraptions of yours." Baggs pointed at the web of copper tubes and silver threads spread between the tables and desks of the first floor. The tangle wound around myriad chalk symbols, colorful crystals, and oddly-shaped beakers, and the front of it seemed to have five or six compasses lined up in a row. The setup looked wonderfully complicated and advanced, but regrettably inert.

"So? Has all this expensive equipment actually done anything?" demanded Goldson.

The cleric and the wizard exchanged a nervous look. MacLeod cleared her throat, and Tarunin stepped forward nervously. "Well, uh, it seems the metaphysical nature of the threat is different from the set of possibilities we originally hypothesized—" began the noctomancer.

"So you didn't catch anything," said Baggs.

"If it had been a straightforward haunting or a demon, the apparatus would have captured it," said MacLeod. "Or detected it at least. But there were no undead or evil spirits here."

"So you didn't catch anything," reiterated Baggs.

Tarunin's shoulders fell in defeat. "No, sirs. The traps are empty."

"You assured us it was a simple haunting!" snapped Goldson. "You said it was certain that this was just the angry ghost of some old sod altering our dreams when we slept here!"

"Well, ah, sirs, your story bore all of the classic signs of a textbook dream manifestation of a common haunting," said the noctomancer.

"We have other theories," added Macleod. "It could have been a divine agent, perhaps of Mordo Ogg himself, or a shared hallucination, or even possibly the… spirits… are what… they said…" She trailed off nervously as she noted the shift in Goldson and Baggs's countenances.

"Do you really think we care for your theories?" barked the old Dwarf. "Every time the Ghost of Mordo Ogg's Day Yet to Come shows up, he gives us predictions that help increase our bottom line by millions of giltin!"

"Hundreds of millions!" said Baggs. "These supernatural visits are the most profitable meetings we ever have!"

"And we could be having them nightly if you two had been competent enough to capture the spirits!" shouted Goldson.

"Sirs, this work is highly theoretical," protested Tarunin. "We didn't capture the spirits on our first attempt, but at least we learned much from the experiments. Next time—"

"The next time the spirits will visit this office is at least a year away, and maybe one or two beyond that if the pattern of the past decade has been any indicator!" snapped Baggs.

"There may not be a next haunting, for all we know!" said Goldson.

"There certainly won't be for you," Baggs added. "You are hereby relieved of your duties."

"You're firing us?" said Tarunin.

"I think the past tense is more appropriate here," said Goldson. "Zeerith will show you out."

The Elven warrior nodded and opened the door again.

"You're not firing him too?" asked MacLeod.

"Why would we hold him accountable?" asked Goldson.

"This sort of thing isn't really his specialty," said Baggs.

Goldson nodded at the Elf. "I think he's better suited for bouncing riffraff out onto the street."

"But… but sirs!" protested Tarunin. "What… what about the good cheer I helped you spread today? The kind deeds I saw you do? It's Mordo Ogg's Day after all!"

"We're well aware of the date," said Baggs.

"It's the only reason we paid you double time," said Goldson.

"And waited until the end of the day to terminate your contracts." Baggs handed each of them a dense confection wrapped in checkered cloth. "Have a fruitcake."

MacLeod looked stunned. "You can't—" she began, but quieted when Zeerith's hand moved to his sword.

"We can. Happy Mordo Ogg's Day," said Mr. Goldson. "Stop by the sixth tier payroll office next week to pick up your final cheques."

"Happy Mordo Ogg's Day!" echoed Baggs.

Zeerith followed the unemployed heroes out of the office to the front gate. The wizard and cleric lingered on the street for a few moments, exchanging insults with the Elf, but soon enough the falling snow rushed them off to their own homes. With sighs of relief,

Goldson and Baggs turned their attentions to the desks in their room.

"Useless junk," said Goldson, clearing off a workspace.

"At least we learned much from the experiments," Baggs said in a mocking voice.

"Yes, mostly we've learned whom not to hire to capture those thrice-cursed spirits." Goldson opened his pocket ledger and set it on the table.

"And we've learned that we must sign the lease on this wretched old office for another five years." The old Halfling poured himself a finger of brandy from the liquor cabinet, and another for Goldson when the old Dwarf waved for one.

"Quite." The Dwarf opened a fresh ink pot, dipped an old quill in it, and began to make notes on his figures.

Baggs fetched a ledger of his own and seated himself at the adjacent desk. They worked quietly, their pens gently scribbling across the pages of their books. Fireworks began outside, sending splashes of color into the gray office. The initial blast startled Goldson into blotching a drop of ink on one of his pages, but otherwise they paid the festivities no mind.

Baggs sat up during one of the louder bursts of pyrotechnics. "I say, Mr. Goldson, did you notice that remark by the vision of Freddy Yet to Be? When he met with those horrible lawyers, he suggested our endeavors in Bloodroot would be most successful."

Goldson grunted and gave a nod. "Hmm, yes. We'll have to be sure to press ahead with that initiative."

"I'm working on the plans now." Baggs nodded at Goldson's ledger. "And you? What part of the spirits' visions have you occupied yourself with?"

"The bit that came after we awoke," said Goldson.

"Pardon?"

"I'm planning for next Mordo Ogg's Day."

"A full year in advance?" Baggs smirked and set down his quill. "Why, Goldson, if I didn't know better, I'd say that those spirits have addled your mind with all of this holiday nonsense."

"Not at all, Mr. Baggs," said Goldson, still writing in his ledger. "But they were right about one thing."

"Oh?"

"Mordo Ogg's Day is not just another day." Goldson looked up. "It is a day when the public looks upon every man and business with extra scrutiny. It is a moment when a minor gesture can boost one's esteem disproportionately when delivered according to custom, or a perceived slight against tradition can likewise cut deeper than any such error should. There is no better opportunity to maximize the impact of charitable displays. There is no better time to clear

Goldson Baggs
Group Inc.

away scandal with a bit of holly and some claptrap about peace on Arth."

"I suppose you're right, looking back on today," said Baggs thoughtfully. "If we show a little goodwill toward people around the holiday, they seem to forget how we've treated them the preceding year."

"'Tis the season for investment into public relations," said Goldson.

Baggs grinned and held up his glass. "Gods bless us, every one."

"Something like that," said Goldson, clinking his brandy against the Halfling's.

They drank, and then set back to work in their ledgers. Their scheming lasted long past the end of the roaring fireworks outside, until the moon reached its zenith in a starry sky.

❧

More adventure awaits on Arth.
Goldson and Baggs
are still up to no good in
Orconomics: A Satire

GLOSSARY

Andarun: Capital of the Freedlands, built in a cleft of Mount Wynspar between the Ridge and the Wall.

Arth: A world much like Earth, but with more magic and fewer vowels.

Drakes: Dragon-kin that are much like full dragons, except smaller, weaker, and nowhere near as smart. Drakes still pose a significant threat, however, especially when encountered in their native element.

Dwarf: Dwarves are shorter than Elves and Humans, but as Dwarves stand almost twice as wide at the shoulder and are famous for violent grudges, it's generally best not to mention that. Rigid, industrious, and usually stoic, Dwarves live in massive clanhomes dug under the mountains. To the puzzlement of many of the other races, there are no Dwarven women.

Elf: The most enigmatic of the Children of Light have sharp, angular features but flowing, graceful movements. They live in tree huts, and many of them have accumulated untold wealth. They are immortal and yet innocent, playful yet powerful, whimsical yet wise. Above all, they are infuriating to almost everyone who is not an Elf. Elves all belong to houses, each of which swears fealty to a Great House. Of course, Elven fealty shifts frequently, and so the Elven houses are forever in flux, playing games of intrigue and power.

The Freedlands: The most powerful nation on Arth, the Freedlands is a federation of semi-autonomous city-states. The Freedlands has a small centralized government, ruled by a king set in Andarun, that regulates the powerful guilds, associations, and corporations that do business in the Freedlands and beyond.

Giltin: The currency of the Freedlands, long considered the standard for all of Arth. The common symbol for giltin is G, as in 5G. One giltin is ten silver shillings. One shilling is ten copper cents.

Gnome: Gnomes take as many shapes and sizes as the clouds in the sky. While their legends hold that all Gnomes once shared a common ancestor, the great Gnomish clans have all become their own sub-races. Be that as it may, it's proper to refer to any of them as a Gnome, be they a Halfling or a Tinderkin or a Deep Gnome. Said sub-races are often used interchangeably with clan names. All Gnomes stand shorter than most Humans, and most are shorter than Dwarves.

Goblin: A race of Shadowkin that descended from the lost clans of the Dwarves. Goblins are short, scrawny, potbellied creatures. Their skin is green, their limbs are spindly. Stereotypes say that Goblins excel at little except breeding, at which they are amazing. It's true that a handful of Goblins can become a tribe in just a few years.

Gremlins: A race of Shadowkin with both feline and lizard-like qualities, once known as Clan Remlon, or Moon Gnomes. Gremlins are known for their inquisitive nature, their mastery of bioengineering, and their tenuous grasp of ethics. Over the centuries, they've created a multitude of Gremlin variants, from the acid-spitting Bilebelly Gremlins, to hulking Brute Gremlins, to spry and acrobatic Stablins, and so on. While some scholars have meticulously documented these variants over the years, most people recognize them all as "Gremlins," and accept a wide degree of "surprises" when dealing with them.

Halfling: Halflings are Gnomes of Clan Haughlin. They have round features, pot bellies, and curly brown hair (even on the tops of their feet.) While generally good-natured, Halflings are averse to manual labor, or indeed anything that isn't comfortable. Unfortunately, they're often very comfortable with petty theft.

Heroes' Guild: An international organization of professional adventurers who specialize in monster slaying, treasure acquisition, hostage retrieval, and more. The Heroes' Guild is among the largest and most powerful organizations on Arth. Its wealth rivals that of the city-states of the Freedlands, and even some small countries.

Human: Y'know. Humans. Originally mixed-race men, the first Humans were children of Gnomes and Elves and Sten. In time, they became so common that they married among themselves and spread throughout Arth. Now they are the most populous race of Man, outnumbering all of the old races combined.

Mankind, Man, Races of Man: Legends say the Creator made the four elder races of Man—the Dwarves, Elves, Gnomes, and Sten—to make Arth more interesting, and has regretted it ever since.

Mordo Ogg: The god of death is not associated with any of the races of Man, nor any of the other gods. He guides those who have fallen on to whatever fate awaits them beyond the grave.

Musana: Musana is the Elven goddess of light and life. She encourages purity and grace, and honors simple living. Musana's high ideals make her popular, especially among the Order of the Sun, but many followers often misunderstand her teaching: Musana's most famous stories depict her humbling those followers who think themselves more pious than others. She is twin sister to Alluna, the Elven goddess of the moon.

Noctomancer: A member of the second great order of mages, the Order of the Moon. Noctomancers are Humans and Gnomes that can weave the elements of air, earth, and shadow.

Oppo: Oppo is the god of charity, also associated with the giving of gifts and acts of mercy. His clergy and followers are famous for providing free healing and warm meals to those in need. Oppo is the patron of the Gnomes of Clan Thomten, commonly known as the Tomte.

Scribkin: The Gnomes of Clan Tinkrin, or Scribkin, stand half as tall as most Humans, with stocky builds, bulbous noses, and thick, bushy hair. Industrious and curious, Scribkin are Arth's most innovative inventors, enchanters, and engineers.

Tinderkin: The Gnomes of Clan Kaedrin, Tinderkin are taller than any other Gnomes, standing a little taller than even a Dwarf. They are lithe, graceful figures with sharp, slender features. Tinderkin are nomadic, traveling in small familial bands. They take their name from the fires they build for nightly gatherings, which are often elaborate visual spectacles.

Tomte: The Gnomes of Clan Thomten, or Tomte, are diminutive, standing just under a Human's knee.

Continued next page

Continued from previous page

They're round and squat, with wide smiles, almond eyes, and bristly hair that covers the backs of their hand and tops of their feet. They are mild mannered, soft-spoken, and generous, but when roused to anger, they have a strength that doesn't belong in such small, rotund packages.

Wizard: A title given to male mages. Its counterpart, witch, fell into disuse during the Age of Darkness.

Wynspar: The mighty mountain that Andarun is set inside is riddled with caves, tunnels, dungeons, and various other dark places for monstrous horrors to lurk.

DEDICATION AND THANKS

This book is dedicated to the memory of Charles Dickens. Mr. Dickens was hopelessly idealistic regarding human nature, and in being so he nudged humanity a little closer to the ideal.

ACKNOWLEDGEMENTS AND GRATITUDE

I'd like to thank my readers, listeners, and fans for the notes of encouragement and support they send my way. It makes an immense difference to me.

Courtney Rae Andersson is a great editor to work with, and her attention to detail improved this book immensely.

Tayla Olandim's illustrations for the book aren't just witty and delightful, but they were delivered on tight timeframes as well. You can see more of her work at taylaolandim.com.

A few fans and beta readers secured appearances for characters of their design in this book, and I almost managed to deliver. I appreciate all that these folks have done for me.

The Human cleric Mirnen MacLeod was brought to you by Jasmine Wahlberg.

The Elven warrior Zeerith of House Illistyneth was a character played by Tyler Peterson. The Human noctomancer Avalon Tarunin was based on a character played by Jamie Erwin. Avalon began his illustrious career as a solamancer, but he was hit by a canon; near the end of editing we realized the lore necessitated a career switch.

I'd like to thank all three for their support.

There were other beta readers who did not name characters this time around. Mike Tibbals remains one of my most dedicated lore masters. Steve Thomas of Klondaeg fame provided helpful insights. Aleisha Kirby, Keith Cohan, Christopher Rodgers all saved my day by providing insights and encouragement in a very short window of time. Geoff Griffith did the same, while providing his customary lessons on celestial motion and accurate timekeeping. Keep it coming.

Book Cover Design by ebooklaunch.com. Thanks to Dane and the crew for a fast turn around.

And finally, I'd like to thank my family, especially my wife. Their patience makes my work possible. Their support makes it worthwhile. Thank you all.

www.ingramcontent.com/pod-product-compliance
Lightning Source LLC
Chambersburg PA
CBHW030532310726
48979CB00010B/1886/J
9780990859673